COUSIN CAMP
CHRONICLES

The Ascent

BOOK 1

Saved By Story

Cousin Camp Chronicles
Book 1 | The Ascent

Published by
Saved By Story Publishing, LLC
Prescott, AZ
www.SavedByStory.house

Cover Design by Alyssa Coelho
Interior Design by Alyssa Coelho
Illustrations by Brylee Allred

Paperback ISBN: 978-1-961336-19-3
eBook ISBN: 978-1-961336-20-9

Printed in the United States of America

www.savedbystory.house

To my kids and grandkids.
Thank you for being brave and courageous,
especially when it was difficult,
and always coming along with Mima
on all of her crazy adventures.

My world shines brighter with all of you in it!

Table of Contents

Load 'em Up!

"I think we're just about ready to roll." Papa winked at Mima as she stacked the last food tote into the back of his blue, four-wheel drive pickup truck.

"Great! Let's get the girls!" Mima's voice was full of excitement as she hurried back into the house.

Maddie, Charlie, and Sophi were finishing their lunch when Mima announced, "All loaded." Realizing that all of their mouths were still full, she began clearing the peanut butter, jelly, and grapes from the table while they finished their final few bites.

"You girls ready?" Papa's eyebrows raised in concern when he saw all the dirty dishes and chipmunk-like cheeks full of food.

"Yes!" the girls shouted in muffled **unison** as they scrambled to clear their dishes.

A buzz of excitement filled the air, inspiring smiles and speedy movement. This was the first camping trip that Maddie, Charlie, and Sophi would be experiencing with just Mima and Papa. No parents allowed at Cousin Camp and, with Mima, it was sure to be an adventure!

Watching them with a bit of playfulness dancing behind her eyes, Mima spurred the trio to clear action, "If you girls have your things all packed, head for the truck!"

"Almost, I just need to grab my backpack," responded Maddie as she dropped her dish in the sink full of soapy water. She noticed her cousin, Charlie, was already in the living room, stuffing the last few items into her pack and zipping up her duffle bag. As she rinsed her bowl and put it on the drying rack, Maddie's blue eyes began to twinkle mischievously — a sure sign she was **scheming**.

Keeping one eye on Charlie, Maddie strode **non-chalantly** past the living room toward the front door. As she reached for the doorknob, the oldest cousin smiled and playfully challenged, "Last one in the truck's a rotten egg!" Snatching up her backpack, she darted out the door, her ponytails swinging side to side. Charlie, bag in tow, was hot on Maddie's heels as the screen door slammed loudly behind them.

Diving head-first into the truck, Maddie let out a victorious "Whoo-hoo! I won!" as Charlie climbed in on the other side, hefting her duffle bag up.

"I almost had you! If you hadn't cheated… " Charlie let the sentence fall off, then teasingly warned, "Better watch out! I'll get you next time!"

Maddie **bantered** back with a quick, "We'll see about that!"

"Just because you're older doesn't mean you always have to win!" quipped Charlie begrudgingly.

Back in the house, Maddie's five-year-old sister, Sophi, was upset.

"That's not fair," she pouted as she balanced on the stool near the sink, trying to reach the sudsy water. "Maddie always wins!"

Placing a kiss on her small blonde head, Mima helped Sophi finish up.

When everything was in order, they clasped hands and made their way to the truck.

"One day, you'll be faster than both of them and then they better watch out!" Mima whispered before she gave Sophi a boost over Charlie's legs and into the middle seat.

A big grin spread across the little one's face, showing Mima her appreciation for always knowing how to make things better.

"Everyone in, seat belts on, and ready to go?" Papa turned the key, letting everyone know it was time.

A chorus of "Yeessss, Papa!" filled the air.

"Let's go have some fun!" Mima cheered as they pulled out of the driveway and began the journey up the mountains.

Making Camp

"She'll be coming round the mountain..." sang the girls and Mima as the city disappeared behind them and rolling hills grew before their eyes.

"Join us, Papa," encouraged Charlie.

"I only sing solo," Papa countered with a deep chuckle. "So low that no one can hear me!"

The girls giggled at Papa's joke.

"You're such a tease," laughed Mima.

The hills turned to mountains as the truck steadily climbed the mountain pass with all of its twists and turns.

"Here comes a tunnel!" announced Charlie. "Hold your breath and touch the ceiling! Ready, set, GO!"

All five passengers inhaled deeply and touched the top of the truck as they entered the mouth of the tunnel.

"Whew…" they all exhaled in unison a full fifteen seconds later as they exited the other side.

"That's hard work," sighed Sophi. "I'm hungry! Is it snack time yet?"

"Mima always has snacks!" The girls smiled when she pulled out her secret stash. Winking back at them, she held out granola bars, fruit snacks, and almonds.

"Fruit snacks!" Sophi cheered excitedly.

"That works," agreed Maddie.

"Ooohh… I like this kind!" Charlie reached for hers. "They have juice in them! YUM!"

Chewing and smacking contentedly from the back seat, the cousins looked out their windows and savored their snacks as the miles rolled by.

A half hour passed before Papa piped up, "Okay, ladies… keep an eye out for our turn-off. We're looking for 'Seven Bridges Campground.' It should be coming up soon."

"There it is!" whooped Charlie a few moments later.

"I see it," Maddie **affirmed** as she lowered her latest book into her lap.

"OH… there it is," Sophi chimed as Papa turned toward the campground's entrance.

Everyone leaned forward, scouting the landscape to see what excitement awaited them. Spring spread out before them in all her glory, her leaves bursting on the trees and flowers displaying their colorful **array** of purple, yellow, pink, blue, and white petals unfolding in the warm sun. Birds sang their melodious songs of welcome.

"Watch out, Papa!" Sophi screamed in her high-pitched squeal, startling everyone as Papa narrowly missed a small brown lizard scooting across the road.

"We are in nature," said Papa, taking a deep breath. "We must be aware of all creatures. Lizards are just the beginning! Remember there could be snakes up here as well as bears, bobcats, and mountain lions."

"We don't want you to be afraid. Just cautious." Mima instructed them calmly, "Make sure you take a buddy with you when leaving the campsite." Glancing at the two older girls, she added, "And don't leave anyone behind!"

"You know… like me!" Sophi added knowingly as they all climbed out of the truck.

"Let's figure out the best spot for your tent," Papa suggested, tugging playfully on her long, blonde ponytail.

The girls all huddled around Papa as he **canvassed** the campsite.

"What about over there under the trees?" offered Charlie, running to an open area under several sprawling Ponderosa pines. She had never been camping before and was not sure exactly what to look for.

"I don't know." Maddie knelt down. "There are a few rocks poking up out of the ground and a tree root shooting out. Won't that be hard to sleep on?"

Maddie and Sophi had been on several campouts with their dad, but they usually slept in a pop-up camper. A tent was going to be a new experience for all three girls. It was part of Mima's plan to have a real camping experience. No "glamping" this trip, much to Papa's **chagrin**.

"Look here." Bending down next to Maddie, Mima moved some dirt around and the small rocks popped loose. "I think with a little preparation, this could be a great spot for your tent. We *are* in the Rocky Mountains, so there probably isn't going to be a place where there aren't a few rocks and roots. Besides, the trees will provide some much needed shade from the sun so your tent doesn't get too warm during the day. Nice job, ladies! This is a great choice."

"How about we get the site ready while Papa grabs the tent for us?" Mima glanced at the girls and then beamed up at Papa.

Taking his cue, Papa **sauntered** toward the truck, returning a few minutes later with the tent, tarp, stakes, and a tool.

"What's this?" Charlie asked, awkwardly struggling to pick up a hammer-shaped tool. "It's kinda heavy!"

"That's a rubber mallet. We'll use it to pound in the stakes," explained Papa.

Sophi, lover of snacks and meat of any kind, blurted, "I thought we ate steaks?"

Giggling, Maddie teased her sister, "Not steaks that you eat, silly!" She grabbed one of the long pieces of pointed plastic Papa had laid on the ground. "This kind of stake."

"Ohhh." Sophi blushed softly. Then straightening her shoulders, she declared, "Well, I like the other kind better!"

"Oh, Sophi," Mima snickered. "You're making me hungry with all this talk of food. We'll make dinner soon, but let's lay out the tent first, so Papa can show you how to hold it in place by driving the stakes into the ground."

After they laid the tarp on the forest floor, Mima pulled the tent out of its bag and began unrolling it.

"Each of you grab a corner and let's lay it out on top of the tarp with the door flap facing into the campsite."

"Why do we put it on the tarp?" Charlie probed.

"That's a great question. Do either of you know?" Papa looked toward Sophi and Maddie.

"Maybe it makes the rocks softer," offered Sophi, not wanting to be left out of the conversation.

"Don't be ridiculous!" Maddie taunted. "Won't it keep the bottom of the tent dry?"

"That's right," Papa **concurred**, casting a cautionary look in Maddie's direction, silently letting her know that she shouldn't make fun.

Sophi quickly stuck out her tongue to let Maddie know she saw and agreed with the quiet communication from Papa.

The girls watched as Papa and Mima placed the poles in position to hold the tent upright.

"Now, it's time to secure it." Papa rubbed his hands together in anticipation. "Who's ready to help with those stakes?"

"Me, me, me!" cried Sophi. "Me first!"

"Okay," Papa **chortled**. "I'll pound in the first two and you can take turns doing the rest." He showed them how to stake down opposite sides, keeping the tent **taut**. Then with dark brown eyes twinkling, he handed the mallet to Sophi. "Okay, your turn. Be careful and don't hit your fingers."

Picking up the stake with one small hand and placing it through the loop, just like Papa had shown her, she hefted the mallet with the other and began gently tapping the top of the stake.

"You're going to have to hit it harder than that," encouraged Papa.

Sophi gripped the mallet more firmly and smacked the top of the stake once, twice, three times. Each smack of the mallet drove the stake further into the ground. With a couple more whacks, the stake was firmly **embedded**.

"Ha ha, Papa!" Sophi held up her arm for all to see her bicep.

Papa reached over and squeezed her small arm.

"Sure enough! Look at those big muscles you have!"

"I'm next," announced Maddie as Sophi finished pounding her last stake into the ground.

Pulling the tent tight, Maddie swung hard and caught the side of the stake, nearly hitting her hand and pushing the stake to the left.

"Dang," she muttered, straightening it and winding up again.

Maddie swung a second time, overcompensating and landing on the other side, skimming the other side of her hand in the process.

"Ouch! This is harder than it looks." Frustrated, she grumbled as she shook her hand to ease the pain.

Mima watched Charlie from a distance as she nervously chewed on her fingernails.

Papa stepped closer and, leaning down, he wrapped Maddie's small hand gently in his giant one.

"Let me help you. Be firm, but don't try to kill it." He chuckled as they planted the stake firmly into the ground together. "Well, we can see you have muscles, too." His eyes twinkled playfully.

Maddie rolled her eyes at Papa and picked up another stake, clearly determined to do this one on her own. Moments later, she had successfully hammered the other two securely into the ground. Proud of herself, she stood up and handed the mallet to Charlie.

"Your turn!"

Charlie **tentatively** reached for the heavy tool while glancing toward Mima.

"You've got this," Mima encouraged. "I believe in you!"

Moving to the next loop and placing the stake in the hole, Charlie took a deep breath, raised the heavy tool, and let it fall onto the head, driving the stake partway into the ground on the first try. A huge grin of accomplishment spread across her face as she finished pounding it securely into the earth.

With one stake firmly grounded, she **resolutely** snatched up the other two stakes and, with a few additional swings, had them both securely planted and her job completed.

"Hurray!" the girls exclaimed as Charlie straightened up and handed the mallet back to Papa.

Unzipping the tent flap, they bustled inside to check out their handiwork.

"Don't forget to take your shoes off at the door," Mima instructed. "But first, why don't you get your bed rolls and duffle bags from the truck and set them up inside?"

Giggling, the girls skipped off together to grab their belongings while Mima set up a small tent that would keep the food safe from most animals that might wander through their campsite.

Looking up from where she was busily preparing their outdoor kitchen, Mima saw Charlie and Maddie returning with bags and backpacks slung over their shoulders, sleeping bags in hand, chattering on about who would sleep where.

"Didn't you forget some…?" Mima was interrupted by a loud cry coming from near the truck.

Tornado Troubles

Mima dropped the bowl she was holding and ran to the truck where she found Sophi on the ground, her sleeping bag unrolled to one side and suitcase emptied of all its toys, blankets, and stuffed animals. Head in hands, the little one sat cross-legged in the middle of her scattered treasures, sobbing.

Mima was already kneeling next to Sophi when the rest arrived at the scene.

"Did a tornado come through here and I missed it?" Papa asked sarcastically, stifling a grin.

Glaring through her tears, Sophi choked out, "It wasn't a tornado, Papa! It was Maddie!" Sniffling, she turned and buried her head in Mima's shoulder.

"I didn't mean to bump her," defended Maddie. Pointing to the mess, she added, "But I didn't do all of this."

Sophi was ready to counter attack when Mima stepped in, "Maybe you did or maybe you didn't, but how might this outcome have been different had you and Charlie made the choice to stop and wait for Sophi?"

Seeing things were under control, Papa headed back to finish putting up the second tent while the girls contemplated their actions.

"Her stuff probably wouldn't be all over the ground." Charlie dug the toe of her shoe into the soft dirt.

"Yeah," mumbled Maddie. "And we would probably be having fun in our tent right now."

"Or eating!" chimed Sophi.

"Those sound like much better ways to spend our time." Mima gently pulled Sophi away from her and looked into her big blue eyes still damp with tears. "Ms. Sophi, what could you have done differently to save yourself all these tears?"

Looking sheepishly at Mima, she whispered as she shrugged her shoulders, "I don't know…"

"You're a smart girl," Mima assured. "I'll bet you can come up with a good one."

Knowing she wasn't going to get out of answering, she let out a deep sigh, thought for a moment, and then replied, "Maybe… ask for help?"

"That sounds like a great idea." Mima smiled, encircling her in a warm embrace and lifting her to her feet. Brushing off her pants, she took in the scene around her and teased, "Looks like you brought your entire bedroom with you. I hope you have clothes in there too."

"Oh Mima, I couldn't leave without my weighted blanket," countered Sophi, "or my stuffed animals, Catey the cat and Tessa the tiger, or my kindle, and my favorite picture of Briea. Oooh and I could never leave my owl, Owlet, behind…"

"Okay already." Mima laughed. "No wonder your bag was so heavy! I don't know how you stuffed all that in, but maybe," she glanced at the older girls, "Maddie and Charlie will help you pick it up and carry it to the tent."

Looking at each other knowingly, they both nodded their heads in agreement and began to help Sophi gather her things.

"Fabulous! You ladies organize your things inside the tent and I'll finish putting together our kitchen. When you're finished, you can help me fix dinner."

"DINNER!" cried Sophi. "I'm starving!"

Lifting Sophi's chin, Mima lovingly chided, "You, my dear, are always starving. If you stuffed this bag the way you like to stuff your face, it's no wonder you managed to make all of this fit into such a small space!"

Looking offended and trying to keep from smiling, she bantered back, "Awww, Mima!"

"What are we having?" Charlie wasn't typically a fan of Mima's choice of food.

"Hotdogs over the campfire."

"Yippee!" Surprised and delighted, all of the girls jumped up and down excitedly, nearly knocking each other over.

Mima chuckled softly to herself.

"Afterward, I thought I would introduce you to one of my favorite camp games!"

"What is it?" Maddie was nearly out of breath.

Mima shrugged her shoulders and taunted, "All I can tell you is that it has to do with food!"

Scrutinizing Charlie to see if maybe she understood this cryptic code, Maddie asked the question on everyone's faces, "What kind of game has anything to do with food?"

Mima shrugged her shoulders as if to say, *Wouldn't you like to know!*

"Food! Food! Food!" chanted Sophi **emphatically** while she marched around in a circle and thrust her hand higher into the air with each shout.

"Give us a hint," begged Charlie over the noise.

Momentarily ignoring the request, Mima repeated herself, "You girls start moving this tornado to your tent, please." Half-way to the outdoor kitchen, she glanced over her shoulder, "It might have something to do with rabbits." Seeing this last clue had totally stumped the girls, she walked briskly away, leaving the three cousins in a **quandary**.

They stared wide-eyed at each other until Maddie broke the silence, "It's always an adventure when we're with Mima, but what kind of game includes food and rabbits?"

Silly Shenanigans

Turning their attention back to the task at hand, each girl grabbed an armload of Sophi's belongings and trekked back toward the tent.

Mima continued setting up the kitchen while she watched the girls make several trips, chattering and talking like a bunch of squirrels.

When she finished, Mima decided to check on the cousins' progress. Nearing their tent, she could hear their debate over who was going to sleep where and who was taking up the most space.

"Poor Sophi," Mima whispered to herself, "It's tough being the youngest."

She eavesdropped on the conversation for a few minutes, enjoying their banter and impressive problem-solving skills, before announcing herself.

"Knock, knock. Anybody home?"

The flap of the tent flew open and Charlie's captivating chocolate brown eyes and smile met her.

"Welcome to our lovely home." Her hand gestured for Mima to enter.

Immediately, giggles from the other two filled the tent.

"Why, thank you," Mima graciously replied as she removed her shoes before entering their domain. Much to her surprise, all three girls had their sleeping bags rolled out and pillows neatly placed on top.

It was obvious whose bed roll belonged to whom. Maddie had her flashlight and latest book set next to her pillow, ready for late-night reading. Charlie had Pink Monkey, Lamb-Lamb, and her favorite blanket on her bag. And Sophi had stacked all of her stuffed animals, blanket, kindle, and other **paraphernalia** next to her bed in a long, winding pile.

Complimenting them on their accomplishment, Mima turned.

Seeing she meant to move the partition and enter the additional room, all three of the girls cried out, "No, Mima! Don't go in there!"

But it was too late. Mima had already caught sight of the result of some sort of explosion of gear, toys, and clothing scattered like **shrapnel** from one side of the tent to the other.

"Oh my goodness! What happened here?" Mima gasped in mock astonishment. "It looks like you girls all brought your bedrooms with you!" Amused and shaking her head resignedly, she exited the tent and went to check in with Papa.

Having set up the adult tent, complete with cots, Papa had decided the time was right for a campfire.

"You're just in time! Want to help me find some kindling?"

Giving Papa a smile and a wink, Mima began gathering several small, dry sticks, leaves, and a bunch of dead pine needles. Before long, they had a roaring campfire.

Hearing the fire crackling and popping, the girls emerged from their tent and made their way toward the warm glow.

"Hey there, girls. Perfect timing! I was just going to call you to come help. Follow me."

The three girls eagerly fell in line behind Mima.

"You look like a momma duck with her three little ducklings," chortled Papa.

"Quack, quack, quack, quack," replied Mima and the girls as they waddled duck-like toward the kitchen.

After setting the table with plates and utensils, Mima sent the girls back to the fire pit to roast their hotdogs while she finished setting out the chips, potato salad, and fixings.

"How are those hotdogs coming along?" she called as she grabbed the buns and sauntered toward the fire. "Anyone ready for a bun?"

"I am!" Charlie enthusiastically held up her skewer and her charred meat.

"Wow, that hotdog is definitely well done!" Mima exclaimed.

Charlie grinned ear to ear, boasting, "It's perfect! Just the way I like them!"

"This takes SO long," moaned Sophi. "I could've eaten two hotdogs by now!"

Everyone smiled, knowing she was probably right.

Soon they were gathered around the table eating, joking, and having fun.

"Look," whispered Sophi loudly, pointing in the direction of a big bunch of bushes. "There's a bunny over there!"

Poking its nose out from the center of the bush, his whiskers twitched as he sniffed the air and checked for danger.

"Ohhh!" whooped Charlie as the bunny turned tail and ran. "He was adorable!"

Maddie shrieked, "Ohh, Mima! What was that game you were going to teach us that has to do with food and rabbits?"

"I'm surprised it took you so long to ask," Mima smirked smugly. "You probably won't like it. It's kind of a boring game." A smile threatened to creep across her face as the girls all protested at once.

"But you promised!" Maddie insisted.

"Uh… that's not fair," Charlie grumbled.

In a last-ditch effort, Sophi desperately added, "Oh, come on. It can't be boring if it has to do with food!"

In sudden support of Sophi, both girls shouted, "Yeah!"

All three begged in unison, "Please, Mima!"

Unable to contain herself any longer, Mima gave in.

"If you insist…" A big smile crossed her face as she stood up and reached for a bag of marshmallows.

"Yum, marshmallows!" squealed the girls.

"Here's the way this works." Opening the package of large marshmallows, Mima pulled one from the plastic bag. "You put a marshmallow in your mouth and say, 'Chubby Bunnies.'"

"That sounds pretty simple." Maddie shrugged.

"You would think so…" Mima paused momentarily. "But the trick is, you aren't allowed to chew it. You have to let it sit in your mouth while everyone takes a turn. The goal is to see how many marshmallows you can fit in your mouth and still say 'Chubby Bunnies' without letting any goo escape your lips."

"That's not so hard." Charlie's tone was smug.

Mima glanced at Charlie.

"Keep in mind that once everyone has done it with one marshmallow, we go around again, repeating the process with a second marshmallow, then a third…" Her voice trailed off for a moment. "Anyone want to play?" She held up the bag of marshmallows.

"Oh, that sounds like fun!" Maddie was the first to cheer, but the other two quickly added their enthusiasm to the mix.

They all decide that Papa should go first. Preferring to be the bystander to all of Mima's **antics**, he made a **gallant** attempt to **thwart** the cousins' efforts. Eventually, they wore him down.

"Come on, Papa!" All three pairs of eyes pleaded. "It won't be the same without you!"

Exhaling deeply, Papa **conceded** and grabbed a marshmallow from the bag Mima had set on the table.

Placing it in his mouth, he started the game as enthusiastically as he could muster, "Chubby Bunnies."

"Now don't chew, Papa! That's the rule!" Sophi reminded him.

"Let the game begin!" **clamored** Charlie. Reaching for her marshmallow, she arranged it daintily in her mouth and repeated, "Chubby bunnies!"

Making it through the first round with each of their marshmallows intact, they began round two. Papa grabbed his second and strategically placed it in his cheek. "Chubby bunnies."

And so it went. They managed to make it through round two with minimal drool escaping, although Sophi and Charlie started to lose control of their giggles, drawing the rest of the players in with their **contagious** play.

"Don' make mee lafff," demanded Charlie in her best stern laughing voice. Third marshmallow in place, she slurred, "Chobbee bonnies."

By the time they reached Maddie's turn, they all had marshmallow goo oozing from their lips and were struggling to speak.

Mouth clamped tightly shut and using her best sign language, Mima motioned, "No chewing," as Sophi, looking like a chubby-cheeked chipmunk, tried to find a vacant spot to put marshmallow number four.

Sticky sludge bubbling out of her mouth and down her chin, she managed to barely squeeze it in.

"Shubbly blunnnniessss," barely left her lips before she broke into a fit of laughter and spewed white goo onto the table, but not before they attacked thin whisps of hair that had fallen out of her ponytail. Maddie and Charlie snickered uncontrollably, holding their hands to their mouths in an attempt to hold in all the ooze.

Mima and Papa's eyes danced at each other, as they watched the cousins' **shenanigans**. Suddenly, a loud snort from Charlie had them all holding their sides, exploding in **merriment** and mushy marshmallows.

With gooey white mush dribbling down her chin and onto her shirt, Mima tore off a handful of paper towels and tossed the rest into the middle of the table.

What's Next?

"That was so hilarious!" whooped Maddie as she wiped the gooey white sludge off the front of her shirt.

Exaggerated snorts and grunts escaped Sophi as Mima washed her face with a wet cloth.

"Hold still, you silly girl," insisted Mima, wiping the last of the sticky from her chin. "Pretty boring game, huh?!"

"That's exactly what I would call it." Papa echoed her sarcasm as he worked harder than everyone else to get marshmallows out of his mustache.

"Yeah, borrring." Charlie nudged Papa playfully. Eyes twinkling, she asked, "Can we play again?"

"I think we've had enough of this game, at least for this evening. Grab the skewers we used for the hotdogs and you can each roast one more marshmallow while we discuss the activities for the rest of the trip."

The sun sank lower in the sky as they regrouped around the fire pit.

"Let's go over our options for the next three days. There's a cave to tour. We could explore the area around our camp. And there's the Ascent that I would really like to hike with the three of you."

"What about Papa?" interrogated Maddie. "Won't he be hiking with us?"

"Not this one," snickered Papa. "These ol' knees just won't let me do all those stairs."

"Stairs?" Charlie's eyes were wide with concern. "How many stairs?"

"A lot!" Mima chuckled as she continued to explain, "The Ascent is a trail that's less than a mile long and is made with old railroad ties. Although it's not a long hike, it does have a lot of **elevation** in that short distance. This means we'll just have to take it slow and steady, and make our way to the incredible views at the top."

"Sophi!" Charlie squawked at the little one lost in her own thoughts. "Your marshmallow's on fire!"

Sophi yanked her skewer out of the fire. Holding up the blackened, disintegrated mass, she burst into tears.

Maddie tried to help and comfort her sister, but Sophi was not to be consoled.

"My marshmallow!" she wailed.

"Oh Sophi," Mima soothed. "You don't have to eat that. Drop what's left into the fire and let's get you a new one."

With the tears all dried and the new marshmallow rotating above the coals, Mima checked in with everyone.

"What are everyone's thoughts for tomorrow?"

Sophi nervously spoke up, "I am not sure about the caves. Aren't they really dark and scary inside?"

"And won't there be bats flying around inside of them?" Charlie's insecurities added to Sophi's, and she seemed grateful to not be alone in her fears of the unknown.

Papa interjected, "The caves we're thinking of are not spelunking caves that you have to crawl through with headlamps. These ones are enormous, with guides that take groups of people in to explore. They have well-lit paths where thousands of people have walked."

"And while there are most likely bats in the caves, they are nocturnal, meaning they only come out when it's dark, usually at night," Mima explained. "With all the light, I would guess there won't be much flying around going on near us."

"Whew," exhaled both girls, letting out the breath they were holding.

"What's there to do here at camp?" Maddie looked around the campsite.

"We brought all kinds of stuff," Mima began. "There's a soccer ball, binoculars, bug catchers, and more."

There was a long pause as the girls silently began contemplating their options.

After a quick moment, Mima added nonchalantly, "Oh… and because I love adventure, I also put together a scavenger hunt we can use to go exploring."

"That sounds like fun!" All three girls concurred, Maddie and Charlie mumbling through their sticky marshmallow chewing and Sophi carefully turning her skewer in an attempt to create a perfectly roasted marshmallow this time.

The girls chattered for several minutes until Sophi shouted, "I think we should tour the cave tomorrow!" With her vote in, she tossed the golden brown marshmallow into her mouth and moaned happily.

Eagerly, Maddie chimed in, "The stairs sound like a fun challenge to me!"

"You would pick that one," grumbled Charlie gruffly. "I think we should stay here and catch bugs, roast more marshmallows, and maybe check out Mima's scavenger hunt."

"Well, it sounds like Papa and Mima will have to decide." Maddie's tone was authoritative after several minutes of debate.

"Oh no!" Papa blurted. "This is your trip. You ladies get to decide."

"But we can't agree," protested Charlie.

"I have an idea," said Mima as she reached for her art supply box. Why don't we write them all down on separate pieces of paper. Then each of you will draw one."

They all decided that would be fair. Mima cut the paper into three even pieces and wrote one activity on each slip of paper. Then she folded them up and put them in a paper bowl.

"Everyone sit at the picnic table, legs out, facing away from me," Mima instructed.

Then she took one straw and, using the scissors, cut it into three different lengths. Placing the three pieces in her hand, so the tops were even, she walked to the other side of the table where the girls had assembled themselves.

"Shortest straw goes first."

"YES!" shouted Charlie, drawing the shortest one. Sophi was delighted that she was not last and Maddie took it all in stride. Since she was the oldest, it wasn't uncommon for her to go last.

Holding the bowl high above the girls' heads, Mima explained the rules.

In turn, they would each pick one of the papers but not look at them until they were given the okay to peek. The first one drawn would be tomorrow's activity. The second one would be the next day's activity, and so on.

"Everyone understand the rules?" Mima appeared to be happy with her plan.

"Yes." The girls' heads bobbed in unison.

Mixing up the papers one last time, Mima nodded for Charlie to make a selection.

With anticipation on her face, she tentatively reached into the bowl and grabbed the first paper her fingers touched.

"Don't look!" Maddie snipped in a motherly tone.

"I'm not!" snapped Charlie.

"Really?" Mima razzed the girls. "Don't be so serious. We'll have great adventures with all of them!"

She lowered the bowl slightly for Sophi who felt around inside before finding one of the papers.

"Looks like this one is yours." Mima put the bowl in front of Maddie to grab the remaining strip.

"Everyone has their paper. On the count of three, you can open them."

The girls' hands were tight with anticipation.

"One… Two… THREE!" shouted Mima and the girls together.

Laughing, they all opened up their hands, each revealing their pick in order.

"I got The Caves," announced Charlie, semi-enthusiastically. "At least it's not the stairs."

"Aww… I wanted that one." Sophi was disappointed. "What does mine say, Mima?"

Mima helped Sophi sound out her words.

"Ssss…cccc…aaa…vvv…eee…nnn…ggg…eee…rrr… Scavenger. Ohh mine is the scavenger hunt!" Sophi cheered.

"That makes mine the Ascent." Maddie beamed. "We saved the best for last, Mima!"

"I am excited to do all of these but I have to admit, Maddie, I'm extremely eager to do the Ascent. I've never done this hike before. It'll be quite the challenge and accomplishment for all of us!"

"Stairs…" muttered Charlie. "Lots and lots of stairs."

"Come on, Charlie! Where's that spunk and curiosity that I love about you?" Mima challenged her granddaughter affectionately.

"It's hiding in the caves," rescued Sophi. "I will help you find it tomorrow!"

Charlie laughed at Sophi's wit, **simultaneously** rolling her eyes in mock disgust.

"You're quite the encourager, Sophi," acknowledged Mima proudly. "It's one of the things I really love about you! Keep up the good work! You just never know who might need an extra bit of encouragement these next few days."

As the moon rose higher in the star-filled sky, Papa stirred the dying embers around and used his best Papa

Bear tone, "Okay girls, it's been a fun day, but it's time for bed."

The three girls sighed as they obediently put their chairs away and trudged off to get ready.

Mima picked up the remaining marshmallows, skewers, and other items that had been left around the campsite and made sure everything was in its place for the evening. Putting the lid on the last tote and zipping the kitchen tent shut, she hollered in the direction of the girl's tent, "I'll be there in five minutes to tuck you in."

"Almost ready," Maddie and Charlie chorused.

"Don't forget to put on dry socks," Mima advised while walking back to where the fire was nearly extinguished.

"Why dry socks?" Sophi peeked out the tent flap.

"They will help you stay warm and dry. Now go get your pajamas on. Mima is on her way!" Papa warned, smiling slyly at Mima.

Scurrying and scuffling noises filled the campsite as the girls hurriedly finished.

They had all just jumped into their sleeping bags when Mima opened the tent door and climbed inside.

"Look at you three, all snug as bugs in a rug."

"Since we're all ready, can we please have a **Konfety Kingdom** story?" urged Maddie.

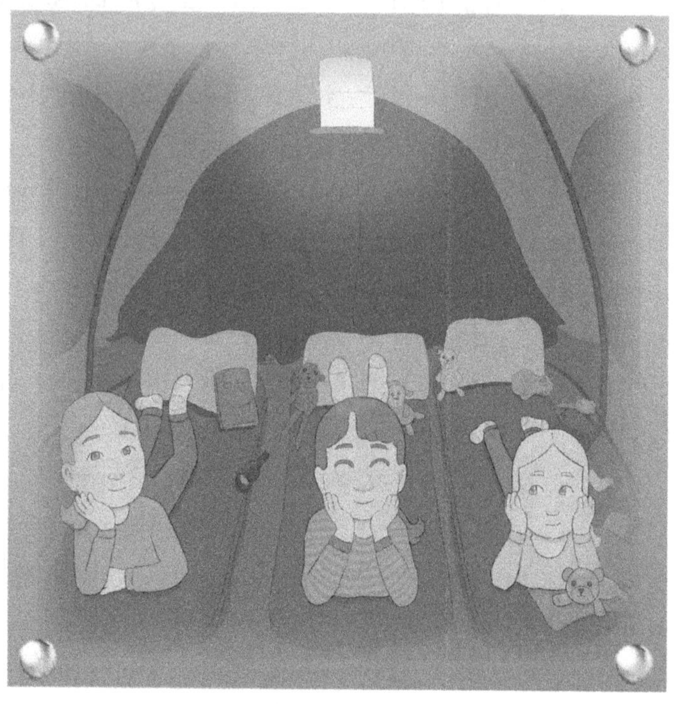

"Pleeeeaaase." Charlie and Sophi added their pleas.

Mima's eyes lit up. She loved creating stories with the girls in their fantasy land, with its flying unicorns and Fairy Kingdom. Along the way, they would discover exciting **phenomena** like rivers flowing with chocolate milk, cotton candy clouds, and paths in the forest made from gumdrops, vanilla wafers, or other tasty treats. They discovered that sugar cookie flower stems made great straws for slurping up the chocolate milk that flowed through the river, and they were always discovering something new like swings made from black licorice ropes or a mountain made of ice cream and sprinkles. There was a new adventure around every delicious rock, tree, or mountain bend.

The girls enjoyed these stories because they helped create them. They never knew where they would go when they started, but they always knew Rosie the unicorn, Jack, and his little sister Jill, and sometimes Rosie's new baby unicorn would all be along for the ride.

"Okay, but we'll need to keep it short. It's getting late and we have a cave to explore tomorrow."

"Maybe Jack and Jill will find a cave." Sophi was beginning to sound sleepy.

"And there are bats inside." Maddie said it with just the right amount of spook.

"But they are nice bats." Charlie smiled wryly.

And so the story began…

The stories these four created could go on for hours and yet always seemed to end too soon. Tonight was no different. As soon as they had started, it seemed, Jack and Jill's cave adventure was winding to a close.

"Jack helped his sister off Rosie's back. After quick hugs with the unicorn and her baby, they skipped off down the hill, calling over their shoulders, 'See you next time Rosie!'"

Mima wrapped up the story and Maddie added the final touch, "The End."

"That was a fun one," yawned Sophi.

"Hmm… What if our cave tomorrow is like the one Jack and Jill found?" Charlie's sleepy eyes sparkled with wonder.

"It might be," winked Mima mischievously, as she pulled the zipper up on Maddie's sleeping bag. "Or it might be even better! You just never know."

With thoughts of what could await them bouncing around in their heads, the girls each said their goodnights and drifted off to dreamland almost as soon as Mima zipped up their tent.

"Sweet dreams," whispered Mima. As she turned toward her tent, she could hear an owl hooting nearby, calling into the night. "And happy hunting to you, Mr. Owl!"

Papa was already sound asleep and snoring loudly.

"No need to worry about bears or bobcats tonight. Papa is snoring loud enough to keep all the nighttime animals away," Mima mused softly as she crawled into her own sleeping bag and closed her sleepy eyes.

Royal Delights

The day had already dawned bright when Mima and Papa awoke.

"Are you ready for the caves?" Papa asked sleepily as he glanced her way.

"I'm ready for anything when we have these kids with us." Mima smiled, happy for this special time together.

"Yeah, I know you are. I'm loving Cousin Camp, and I think they are too." He kissed her forehead before he roused himself out of his cot, readied for the day, and went out to start a morning fire.

Mima quickly got ready and headed to the kitchen area to prepare breakfast.

One by one, the girls emerged, first Charlie and then Sophi.

"What's for breakfast, Mima?" Charlie pulled her jacket on over her pajamas as she moved toward the table.

"Yeah. What's for breakfast? I'm so hungry, I could eat a bear!" Sophi declared dramatically, looking like she couldn't decide between possible food and the warmth of the fire.

"Pancakes and sausage," answered Mima.

Observing Sophi's dilemma, she decided to persuade her in a different direction.

"How about you two girls get dressed now and then help me fix breakfast? Put on a long-sleeved sweatshirt or sweater over your t-shirt until it warms up. You'll need one for the caves today anyway. Oh… and while you're in there, tell Maddie it's time to wake up."

Charlie and Sophi disappeared back inside the tent, where Maddie grunted and groaned in response to the other two coaxing her to get up.

"Stop it!" Maddie screeched.

"She's such a grumpy sleepyhead," pouted Sophi as she stomped out of the tent, Charlie on her heels. "She doesn't like mornings!"

"That may be true, but we have a cave to check out today, so we need to get up." Mima spoke loud enough for Maddie to hear.

"Girls, the sun has been up for hours and the day is half over!" Papa joked as he sat back in his chair and observed his handiwork, the flames reaching up into the cold morning air.

"Oh Papa!" mocked Charlie. "It's only nine o'clock. We haven't even eaten yet!"

"Like I said," Papa scoffed, "the day is half over! Look at all the fun you're missing out on." He swept his hand around the campsite, pointing first to the roaring fire and then the kitchen where Mima had already laid out a breakfast treat.

Following the direction of his hand, the girls gasped with delight when they saw four mugs of hot chocolate steaming in the brisk morning air.

"Hot chocolate! YUM!" Charlie cheered.

"And whipped cream!" Sophi almost **levitated** with excitement, forgetting all about helping Mima as she made a **beeline** for the table where all the fixings were waiting to be added.

"Maddie is going to be sad she missed this." Papa faked a sniffle.

"Missed what?" Maddie rubbed her eyes at the doorway of the tent.

"Oh… nothing," Papa teased, as he picked up the whipped cream bottle and made exaggerated swirls on top of his mug.

When Maddie grabbed her blanket and wrapped it around her, Mima pointed back toward the tent.

"What's the rule at Mima's house?"

"Hmmm…" Maddie thought for a moment. "No breakfast until our beds are made and we're dressed. But, this isn't your house." Her tone was onery as a smile spread across her angel-kissed face.

"Maybe not technically," Mima quipped with a grin of her own, "but the rules still apply. Now, get dressed, and then you can have some with breakfast."

Sophi giggled as she arranged the last of her chocolate sprinkles on top of the cream and took a big slurp of her cooling drink.

"Be careful, young lady." Mima's eyebrows raised in warning before she turned her focus back to the pancakes she was flipping. Charlie and Sophi passed each other a sneaky smirk, unaware Mima and Papa both caught the entire exchange.

Soon Maddie was at the table adorning her drink with a fluffy white hat of whipped cream and Mima was bringing the pancakes and sausage to the table.

"It's a feast fit for a king!" crowed Papa, roostering up as he took the platter from Mima. "And since I'm the only king, it must all be for me!" And with that, he placed the full platter down in front of himself, grabbed a fork, and acted as though he was prepared to eat the entire plate himself.

"Nooo!" Sophi wailed as Maddie and Charlie jumped to their feet, ready to take Papa on for his platter of food, nearly knocking over their mugs in the process.

"Okay, okay," giggled Mima as she took the platter from Papa and motioned for the girls to sit down.

"Now hear this," Mima **conjured** her best royal voice, "King Papa, since you had no intentions of sharing this plate filled with delicious food, you'll have to pay the consequences for your greed. As the preparer of these appetizing **morsels**, I do hereby declare that you will now be the last to eat!" Shooting him a playful wink, she held the platter out of his reach where each of the girls could obtain some **delectable** goodness.

"That's not fair!" Papa harrumphed, folded his arms, and pretended to pout.

The girls were greatly amused by this silliness. It was one of the things that made it so much fun to be with Mima and Papa. They were always teasing each other and having fun, even if they did have a few rules.

As they joked and ate, the sun rose higher in the sky and the air warmed a bit as the cousins gobbled up the last of the food on their plates.

"Get your face out of your plate, Sophi," Mima **chastened** when she saw the little one's strands of hair fall into the sticky goo.

"But it's SO good." Sophi smacked her lips. "I want to get every drop!"

Mima rolled her eyes and smiled. She had a lot of experience with long, sticky hair.

"How about you girls gather all the dishes and trash and put the food away, while I make soapy water to wipe everything off." Mima changed the subject and enlisted her royal subjects' assistance in the **dastardly** duties of clean up.

Ignoring the grumbles and murmurs, Mima set up the wash basin and started whistling the tune of hard-working dwarves in a story they all loved.

Seeing their complaints were getting them nowhere, the girls pitched in. Thirty minutes later, the kitchen was clean and they directed their efforts toward helping Papa put out the fire.

Mima hefted the basin full of soapy water and poured it over the last few flickering embers. "No sense wasting this water."

"Can we go to the cave now?" Maddie's enthusiasm made Mima smile. "Our chores are all done, and I can't wait to scout out the cave!"

The girls all agreed they were ready to head out for the day's adventure.

"Grab your sweatshirts," Mima instructed.

"Why do we need our sweatshirts?" Sophi whined.

"You might want to listen to Mima. She may know something you don't," warned Papa.

When the girls turned to look at Mima, they saw her eyes twinkling with secret knowledge as she shrugged her shoulders, turned, and walked toward the truck.

Snatching up their jackets from the picnic table, they all climbed in behind her and headed out on their first adventure.

Underground Adventures

It was late morning when they arrived at the cave site. The sun was shining and a soft breeze blew as they climbed the hill from the parking lot to the entrance. Entering through the glass doors, they found people buying tickets and eating snacks. Some had just finished their tours, and others waited patiently for their turn to explore.

After making his way to the counter, Papa sauntered back to where they were waiting and held the tickets up for the group to see.

"They start a new tour every twenty minutes," he began. "There are a couple of groups ahead of us, so it will be about forty minutes. We need to listen for group number 276. That's us."

Papa had barely finished when Sophi, eagerly eyeing the plate of a passerby, piped up, "Does that mean we can get some lunch?"

"Let's go see if we can rustle up some of those French fries." Papa beamed. He loved watching the girls' faces light up, and with Sophi, that usually involved food.

He tousled the youngest, hungriest one's hair and signaled for them all to follow his lead.

The cousins trailed Papa, weaving in and out of people to reach the serving line, while Mima **scrounged** up a table where they could sit together and waited for the **entourage** to return.

"That didn't take long." Mima made room on the table as the girls returned with ketchup, utensils, and napkins, and Papa carried a tray piled high with food.

"We got French fries and sandwiches," Charlie tattled.

Mima raised her eyebrows at Papa who shrugged his shoulders and sheepishly admitted, "They twisted my arm."

The girls all laughed.

"Ooohh, Papa's in trouble," Maddie teased while simultaneously reaching for some fries, stopping momentarily to dip them in ketchup on their way to her mouth.

Papa reached over and snatched at her fries, making all three girls giggle and roll their eyes in his direction.

They were talking, laughing, and eating the last bites of their lunch when the announcement came over the loudspeaker, "Group 276… begin gathering at the south entrance. Your tour will leave in five minutes."

Quickly collecting the trash and tossing it into the bin, the **clan** moved toward the designated location.

Excitement played across the three cousins' faces as the tour guide stepped up and began his welcome.

"Good afternoon, everyone! You're standing at the entrance to one of the greatest discoveries of the mid-1800s. A team of speleologists, known as spelunkers, heard through Indian Folklore about a place where the water flowed, created great tunnels, and crafted spectacular displays of **sedimentary** formations. These men went in search of this sacred place and, in 1859, discovered Weeping Widow Caverns. The stories foretold described only a fraction of the beauty they found here below. Today, I will share with you the **elegance** this cave has bestowed upon us. Does anyone have any questions before we ride the elevator down into the cavern?"

Sophi shouted, "What's a slunker?"

Everyone stifled a laugh as the guide smiled down at her inquisitive face.

"This is probably the most frequently asked question. *Spel*unkers," he emphasized the pronunciation, "are people who enjoy exploring caves."

As soon as he finished this explanation, Charlie's hand immediately shot into the air.

"Yes, young lady." He pointed at Charlie.

"Why do they call it 'Weeping Widow'?"

"Another great question! Legend has it that there was a beautiful Indian princess whose love was called off to war shortly after they were wed. She waited patiently for his return through the passing of many moons, until one morning, while on the nearby mountain, she saw a trail of riders far off in the distance."

The girls leaned forward, intrigued by the guide's masterful storytelling.

"She scurried down the mountain, her feet barely touching the ground. The princess alerted everyone to the approaching party with shouts of, 'They're home!' as she ran through the streets to meet the riders who were entering their village. She searched for her beloved husband, finding her father, brothers, and others from the village as they rode in weary and battle-worn; but her love was nowhere to be found."

Charlie gasped, **intuitively** understanding what had happened to the warrior.

"Running to her father, she cried out for him to tell her where her husband had gone. He looked down sorrowfully at his distraught daughter, a tear forming in the great chief's eye. The young princess instantly knew her love was gone. She took off running and disappeared back into the mountains, and was never seen again."

Sophi sniffled and her eyes filled with tears.

"Many generations passed before the day when some children were playing on these same mountains and came across an opening they hadn't seen before. They gathered flashlights and entered the darkened tunnel, following the passageway winding down to where it opened up deep in the belly of the mountain. There they found magnificent formations shaped from the sediment left behind from every droplet of water. According to the legend, the water droplets are the tears the princess cried for her lost love. Those droplets created all the many tunnels and formations you're about to witness, and her tears continue today."

A single tear slid down Maddie's cheek, as if on cue.

"It also tells us that she's never stopped looking for him and that sometimes, even now, if you listen closely, you can hear her soft cries calling out to him on the wind as it gently rushes past."

Charlie exhaled a soft, "Wow…" as she glanced over at Maddie and Sophi. All three girls were **enamored** by the tale, staring intently as the guide finished.

"Shall we go below and see what she has created?" he asked with a bit of mystery in his voice.

The girls shook their heads **affirmatively**.

"The elevator will take us down ten stories, to the edge of the first opening, where you'll see a walkway and stairs winding through each of the areas. Please stay together until I ask you to move on to the next portion of the tour. I don't want to lose any little children today." He smiled playfully as he motioned for them to step into the elevator.

Maddie and Charlie looked at each other with curiosity and Sophi scurried to Mima, her big blue eyes wide, and quickly grabbed her hand.

"It's okay, Sophi. He's just teasing." Mima gave her a gentle, reassuring squeeze. "Besides, Papa and I will keep you safe."

The littlest cousin snuggled in between Papa and Mima as the elevator began its descent.

When the elevator doors opened, everyone noted the sudden change in temperature.

"Brrr… You're right, Mima." Maddie zipped up her jacket. "We do need our jackets."

"It's *much* colder down here," agreed Charlie.

As they traversed the walkways in the cavern, they learned something new at each of the exhibits. Charlie and Maddie took turns asking questions about the different formations while Mima and Papa took turns corralling Sophi as she bounced back and forth with all the energy of a five-year-old trying to contain herself in a room full of glass figurines.

"I hate to say it, but it's a good thing the little guys aren't here with us! We'd really have our hands full," Mima whispered to Papa about Charlie's little brothers after pulling Sophi back away from a fragile formation.

"Those **Irish twins** would be over the railing in a flash, and in different directions." He quietly chuckled as he described the possible chaos.

"Does anyone know the difference between a stalactite and a stalagmite?" inquired their leader as they stopped in front of a huge display of icicle-shaped formations.

"I do! I do!" Maddie beamed confidently. "The stalactites hold 'tight' to the ceiling, which means the stalagmites grow up from the floor of the cave."

"Nicely done!" The guide clapped his hands together. "Have you been to a cave before?"

"No." Maddie snickered. "Mima told us on the way here!"

"Cheater!" Sophi wrinkled up her nose and made a snide face.

"It's not cheating. It's just good listening!" Maddie playfully defended herself against the accusation.

They continued down the walkway to a set of stairs and to the next display where they learned about the different formations like columns, lily pads, and **soda** straws, and how to tell the difference between each of them.

"You should never touch the formations." The guide wriggled his fingers in the air, making sure he had their attention for this important information. "The oil from your skin will block the water and stop the formation from growing."

The girls nodded in understanding.

"Whoa! Look at that! It looks like a spider web!" Sophi pointed at an amazing formation of crystals hanging high in the cave. "You don't have to worry about anyone touching that one!"

They learned how the inside of the cavern was more than one hundred feet tall in some areas and shorter in others where the water had worn down the limestone in the rock to create bridges and tunnels.

"Do you hear that?" Charlie cocked her head to one side.

"It sounds like water, or maybe it's the wind!" Maddie mused. "I wonder if it's the princess calling for her husband?"

It was so quiet, you could hear a pin drop as they all listened intently for the weeping widow's voice, but all they heard was the wind passing through the tunnel and drops of water as they landed on the nearby stalagmites.

Having finally settled down, Sophi was enjoying the tour while keeping her eyes on the cave's ceilings.

Eventually, her curiosity got the better of her and she had to ask, "Are there bats in this cave?"

The guide kneeled down eye-level with Sophi, and pointed up to the ceiling where black markings appeared on the wall.

"See the black against that limestone wall?"

Sophi squinted her eyes and followed his finger.

"Oh yeah! Is that bat poop?"

"Yes." The man chuckled at Sophi's disgusted tone. "However, bat droppings are called guano."

"Ew… that sounds like a disease!" Maddie wrinkled up her nose. "So, where exactly are the bats?"

"I was going to ask him that!" Sophi crossed her arms **dejectedly**.

"I'm sure you were, young lady," he encouraged the bouncy child. "You're very astute!"

Proud of herself, Sophi stood a little taller before she wondered, "What's astute?"

The adults all smiled as Mima answered, "That means you're smart."

Sophi threw back her shoulders proudly.

"Thanks! Now, how about them bats?"

The guide's eyes twinkled with the magic of the conversation as he stood up.

"They've been around us this entire time. More than likely they're high above, sleeping in their roosts.

Bats cannot see, so they do not need the light. Instead, they make a high-pitched sound when they fly. This sound **reverberates**, creating an echo when it bounces off of objects, helping them to steer clear of anything in their way."

"How do they fly so high?" Charlie craned her neck to see up into the dark recesses of the cave's upper walls.

"Did you know that bats are the only mammals that can fly? Some can fly as high as a bald eagle, up to ten thousand feet. These walls aren't nearly that high, so they can fly to their roosts with ease."

All too soon, they found themselves at the end of the tour and their guide bidding them farewell.

"Thank you!" Everyone waved goodbye as they turned to leave.

"That was so much fun!" Maddie's grin said it all as she climbed into the truck.

"Was it ever!" Charlie beamed.

"Yeah! And it wasn't scary at all! Except when I thought he was serious about losing little kids." Sophi shivered at the thought. "But now I know he was just teasing us."

"But…" Charlie paused. "We never heard the sound of the widow calling to her love."

Roll 'em Up

Once back at camp, Mima fixed a snack to hold them over until dinner.

"Anyone want to play soccer?" Maddie tossed a soccer ball into the air and juggled it several times with her feet.

"As long as you don't play Keep Away from me!" Sophi put her hands on her hips for **emphasis**.

"How about if we make a triangle and kick it back and forth? Maybe Papa will join us." Charlie looked at Papa, her big brown eyes pleading with him to accept her invitation.

Papa laughed.

"Maybe, but I am going to have to start our campfire first. I think Mima needs it for our dinner this evening."

"What's for dinner?" Maddie looked toward the kitchen where Mima busily gathered supplies.

"I thought you might like to make pizza rolls." Mima set the supplies on the picnic table.

"Yesssss!" Sophi exclaimed as she kicked the ball. "How do you make pizza rolls?"

"With tortillas, pizza sauce, cheese, and toppings like pepperoni, pineapple, bell peppers, black olives, and mushrooms."

"You can keep the bell peppers and mushrooms." Sophi turned up her nose. "But I like pepperoni!"

"Meat-eater!" Maddie teased, launching the ball in Charlie's direction.

"I love all pizza toppings because I LOVE pizza!" Charlie danced around playfully and then chased after the ball.

"Well, it's a good thing I brought all kinds of options and you each get to make your own." Mima headed back to the kitchen for more supplies.

"Hurray!" Sophi jumped into the air. "I can't wait to make mine!"

Soon the fire crackled and popped, and the flames leapt up from the logs as Papa moved them around with a long stick.

"Are you going to join us now?" Maddie nimbly rescued the ball with the toe of her dirty sneaker before it rolled under Papa's chair.

"I'll play for a few minutes while this fire burns down a little. We'll need a good bed of coals if we're going to cook our pizzas without burning them."

"Yay! Papa's going to play!" Maddie dribbled the ball back to her area.

"Come over here by me," enlisted Sophi.

"Right here, Papa." Charlie pointed to the open space between her and Sophi.

Obediently, he took his place between the two girls.

They lobbed the ball back and forth for several minutes, kicking and retrieving.

"Has the fire died down yet?" inquired Mima.

Papa snagged the ball from Maddie and sent it in Charlie's direction before marching over to check on the coals.

"Looks like we have a nice bed of coals here." Papa stirred the fire, making sure there were no hot spots. "I would give it just a few more minutes."

"Does that mean we can make our pizzas now?" Maddie glanced at all the delicious ingredients on the table.

"Looks that way." Mima opened the can of olives and set them next to the mushrooms. "Everyone, wash your hands and come make your pizza."

"Awesome-sauce!" Sophi lunged toward the sink, trying to beat Charlie to the front of the line.

"Hey!" cried Charlie. "That was my foot!"

"Sophi, there's plenty of room and ingredients for everyone to create their pizza roll," chided Mima. "No need to body-slam your cousin on the way to the table. I've laid a piece of foil on the table for each of you. Get a tortilla and place it on your foil."

"We put the sauce on first, don't we?" Charlie reached for a tortilla.

"Correct. Choose one of the sauces. Then add your cheese, and finally your toppings. Make sure you have enough cheese to make it nice and gooey!" Mima added a handful of cheese to her own tortilla.

"I'm using the white sauce, cheese, and lots of chicken." Sophi paused, scrutinizing her handiwork.

"Oh, and pineapple." She tossed several chunks of the sweet fruit onto her tortilla.

"Awesome! I'm so glad you didn't forget the pineapple!" Mima winked.

"Mine is a supreme pizza. It has everything except anchovies." Charlie added a little more cheese to the top.

"Yuck… anchovies." Maddie scrunched her nose and made a sour face.

"Good thing I didn't bring any," Mima laughed. "How about you, Maddie? If you don't want any anchovies, what are you putting on your pizza?" Mima teased as she leaned over to get a better look at Maddie's creation.

"Pepperoni, sausage, and pineapple." Maddie smiled proudly. "Oh! And of course cheese."

"It looks like you ladies have done a magnificent job! However, I think Papa's struggling with his." Mima watched as Papa tried to roll up his tortilla and toppings squirted out both ends.

"Maybe…" Papa attempted to smash it all down as he re-rolled his bulging masterpiece.

"What if you made two of them, instead of trying to get it all on one?" Mima passed the tortillas to Papa.

"Now that sounds like an excellent idea!" Papa opened the bag and pulled out another one.

To prevent the same fate from **befalling** the girls, Mima showed them how to wrap the foil tightly around the pizza roll and write their names on it while Papa redistributed his pile of toppings into two smaller rolls.

With everyone's dinner wrapped and ready to bake, Papa spread the coals evenly in the bottom of the fire pit. Then he set a grate, with short, stubby legs, over them, allowing space for the heat to circulate around the foil, but not be in direct contact with the coals, which might cause them to burn. They all put their pizza rolls onto the fire grate and waited.

Mima reached for the tongs and they took turns rotating their pizzas, ensuring they would be warm all the way around.

It didn't take long before the cheese was bubbly hot and ready to eat.

"Be careful when you open the foil." Mima helped Sophi open hers. "There will be steam inside and they could be too hot, so blow on them first to cool them down before you bite into them."

"Oh! They are warm!" Maddie quickly pulled her hands away from the escaping steam.

"These look so yummy!" Charlie took off the last of her foil. "I cannot wait to eat!" She blew gently to cool hers down.

"Will you blow on mine, Mima?" asked Sophi impatiently.

"I bet you can do it yourself." Mima encouraged Sophi while unwrapping her own delicious bundle of goodness.

"But it takes too long." She blew several quick puffs of air to prove her point.

"Oh, Sophi." Mima chuckled. "Don't give up so easily! You've got this!"

"Mmm… This is so good." Maddie slurped a piece of cheese stringing from the tortilla to her mouth.

"Finger-licking good." Sophi wiped the sauce from her chin with her hand and sucked it off her fingers.

"Totally awesome," agreed Charlie, leaning her head back and dropping the last of the tortilla into her open mouth.

"These were pretty good," Mima admitted as she ate the last of hers.

"It is pizza!" stated Papa. "How do you go wrong with pizza?"

They laughed together as they finished their meal.

"How about some help cleaning while Papa stokes the fire?" Mima began clearing the dishes.

The girls all pitched in without a word of complaint and soon they were all sitting by the fire with chocolate chip cookies.

"Hey… Where's mine?" Papa looked dejectedly at the girls.

"You didn't help with dishes." Maddie took a bite from one of her cookies and taunted Papa with a smile.

"But he did rekindle the fire." Mima handed him some cookies.

"At least one person appreciates my fire skills." Papa sniffed, looking to see if the girls were paying any attention to him.

"Oh, Papa!" they all cried in unison.

He smiled with satisfaction as he leaned back in his chair and took a papa-bear sized bite out of his cookie.

Stargazing Wonders

As they sat around the campfire, the sun sunk low behind the mountains and the stars began to shine.

"I can't believe all these incredible stars out here!" Maddie's voice was full of wonder.

"Yeah," Charlie concurred. "It's like someone opened a container of glitter and tossed it into the sky!"

"That's a great way to describe it," acknowledged Mima, lifting her gaze heavenward.

"Oh, oh! There's the Big Dipper!" Charlie pointed excitedly toward the group of stars.

"Nicely done," Papa congratulated.

"Where's the Little Dipper?" Maddie stared intently at the night sky. "Isn't it near the Big Dipper?"

"You're right, Maddie." Papa stretched his hand heavenward. "It's close by. Do you see the Big Dipper Charlie pointed out?"

"Yes," Maddie responded enthusiastically.

"Where? I don't see it." Sophi spun around and fell to the ground in a heap.

"Come sit with me, Sophi. I'll help you find it," Mima encouraged softly.

Sophi moped as she shuffled over.

"Oomph!" exhaled Mima as Sophi plopped herself in her lap. "Goodness, Sophi!" She took a deep breath. "You almost broke my lap!" she teased, giving the child a warm hug.

"Now, look right over there." Mima tilted her head in the direction of the Big Dipper. "Do you see that big spoon in the sky?" Then, realizing her error, she corrected herself, "Actually, it's more like a ladle or a big scoop. Something you might use to dish soup out of a pan, rather than a spoon."

Sophi squinted up at the stars.

"I see it! I see it!" she shouted proudly.

"See how there are two parts to the Big Dipper?" Papa asked. "There's the handle and there's the ladle."

"I see them both," said Charlie. "How about you, Maddie? Do you see both pieces?"

"I sure do."

Stretching her hand up and pointing with her finger, Mima outlined both portions of the constellation for Sophi.

"If you go to the edge of the scoop," Papa continued, "farthest from the handle, there are two stars that make up the outside of the ladle."

"Ah-hm," the girls murmured, letting Papa know they had followed his directions.

"These two stars are sometimes called The Pointers, because they point to the North Star, and the North Star is the first star in the handle of the Little Dipper."

There was a pause while the kids all searched the sky for the North Star.

"There it is," reported Maddie.

"I found it too," Charlie chimed.

"Got it!" Sophi announced triumphantly.

"Good job, ladies." Mima congratulated their fast achievement with a round of applause. "Did you also know that when you're facing the North Star, you're actually facing in a northerly direction?" The girls stared open-mouthed at Mima as she continued, "It's true! Long ago, sailors used the North Star at night and the sun during the day as a compass to help them stay on course, out on the open seas."

"That's cool!" Maddie looked dreamily skyward.

"Would you like to know some more about the stars?" questioned Papa.

"Sure!" Charlie appeared totally captivated by this new information.

"There are some star patterns, like the Big Dipper, that are not considered constellations."

"What?!" exclaimed Charlie, as all three girls turned abruptly to stare questioningly at Mima.

"Papa's correct! The Big Dipper is actually part of a bigger star pattern, known as the constellation Ursa Major. A part of Greek mythology, Ursa Major means 'Great Bear.'"

The girls had no idea there was so much to learn about those twinkling lights in the sky.

Papa pointed out the rest of the stars making up the Great Bear.

"Did you know that you can see this constellation all year long, but there are others you can't?"

The girls looked at Papa in disbelief and then at each other, as if asking, "Is this one of Papa's trick questions?"

"That's right," Mima confirmed. "There are some constellations that can only be seen in the United States at certain times of the year. The stars like the Big Dipper, and Little Dipper, can be seen all year round because they sit below the horizon and near the North Star."

"Wow! I just thought the stars were pretty. I didn't know you guys knew so much about them." Sophi looked into Mima's eyes with admiration.

"Me neither!" Charlie glanced from Mima to Papa and back up at the sky. "Finding stars and constellations has been really fun!"

"We should find some more." Settling in for more, Maddie tucked her feet up into the chair and hugged her knees.

Papa helped the girls find Draco (in the shape of a dragon) and Cassiopeia (in the shape of a W) before Mima interjected. "We should probably wrap up this star-gazing lesson for tonight. It's getting late and we have a big day tomorrow."

"Oh, Mima!" the girls **sulked**.

"To think, star-gazing could be so interesting." Maddie sighed in wonder.

"Yeah, all I've ever done is watch for shooting stars." Charlie stood and stretched sleepily.

"Ah-hmm," agreed Sophi. "I liked finding the dragon one best."

"Hmm… You like the dragon one, now do you?" Mima had an idea. "What if we add a dragon to our Konfety Kingdom story this evening?"

"Or maybe Rosie can point out some of these constellations to Jack and Jill," offered Charlie.

"Yeah! They can have a star-gazing adventure too," suggested Maddie.

"Hurry!" Sophi excitedly took off toward their tent. "Let's get ready for bed!"

With renewed energy, Maddie and Charlie joined Sophi and dashed off to get ready, leaving Mima and Papa chuckling at their antics.

"This star-gazing was so much fun and not part of our plans at all." Papa held his hand out to hold Mima's.

Nodding in agreement, Mima reached out and smiled as he wrapped his big paw around her little one.

"And I love that they are so excited about helping me add it to our story. We have so much fun creating these adventures together. It's always a surprise what they come up with!"

"I am not sure who enjoys those stories more." Papa smirked. "Your eyes light up every time the girls suggest making one up."

Mima blushed and leaned back in her chair to enjoy a few quiet moments.

Elves and Fairies and Gnomes, Oh My!

"Miimmmmaaaa!" the girls called from their sleeping bags.

"We're ready for our story!" Sophi's high-pitched squeal could be heard throughout the camp and probably by all the creatures in the nearby forest.

"Coming!" Mima answered, as she made her way to their tent.

Taking her shoes off at the door, Mima stepped into the tent lit by the soft glow of a lantern, and found all three cousins lying on their bellies, chins resting on their hands, anticipating the journey they were about to embark upon.

Mima giggled.

"You sure you aren't too tired? It's been quite a long day. Maybe we should wait until tomorrow night." She reached for her shoes as if she might leave.

"Oh no you don't!" insisted Charlie as the other two shook their heads in agreement and all three pulled Mima down onto their bed rolls. "I already have an idea for one of the constellations they can find."

"Well, we had better get going then." Mima nestled onto the ends of their sleeping bags, and began…

Once upon a time, there was a magical unicorn named Rosie. She had two amazing friends, Jack and Jill—a couple of children who were not so different from you and me! They loved adventure and had long ago stumbled upon Rosie, who had been caught in a puddle of soft, sticky taffy, just off the gumdrop trail near the east entrance to Konfety Kingdom.

The more Rosie struggled, the more deeply entrenched into the brightly colored taffy she became. By the time Jack and Jill had found her, the tips of her beautiful white wings were in danger of becoming entangled in the colorful, sticky goo. But, lest we run out of time, let's save the retelling of that story for another day.

Jack and Jill enjoyed spending time with Rosie, exploring Konfety Kingdom with all of its magic and interesting creatures. They never knew who or what might pop up behind a grove of trees or around the next corner.

There were wizards and fairies, gnomes, elves, ogres, and other creatures with special powers that lived in the enchanted land made of various candies and yummy goodness! At any moment, they could emerge from the forest filled with fruit-flavored lollipops, or in the flower fields of scrumptious sugar cookies beautifully decorated with colorful frosting, or on the ice cream mountains, and…

"Don't forget the sprinkles," interjected Sophi.

"We don't dare forget the sprinkles." Mima pretended to drop sprinkles on top of the girls as she continued the story.

Today was the day everyone in Konfety Kingdom had been waiting for, and Rosie was excited that the special day had finally arrived! It had been a long, anxious week for her. And Father Time, it seemed, had slowed time to a crawl, just because he could.

"Mean ol' Father Time!" Maddie made a sour face and then mischievously added, "Just wait 'til the Fairy Princess gets a hold of him. She'll wind him up good!"

Mima chuckled, knowing that Papa could hear them from his perch by the fire and that Maddie's comment had likely brought a giant smile to his face.

"Yeah, she will!" Mima agreed.

Rosie nervously licked the peppermint trunk of a nearby candy cane tree while she waited for the children to arrive. She knew they were making their way up the winding gumdrop trail to their favorite meeting spot at the edge of the candy cane forest and would appear any moment.

The sun was shining brightly, breaking up the low-lying cotton candy clouds, when she saw the top of Jack's and Jill's heads rising up over the edge of the trail.

Rosie stomped her front hooves and let out an excited whinny.

"Hi Jack! Hi Jill!" She danced and pranced excitedly, nearly knocking down one of the smaller candy cane trees.

"Hello, Rosie!" Both children breathlessly greeted their friend and ran the last few steps to her, flinging their arms around her neck and nuzzling in for a hug.

"It's so good to see you again!" Jill stroked her gently on the nose.

"We hurried as fast as we could, but our list of chores seemed to be never-ending," Jack reported. "I hope you haven't been waiting long."

"I haven't been here long enough to eat the entire candy cane tree." Rosie laughed and whinnied. "But I did try to lick off its bright red stripes."

The children and Rosie bantered for a few minutes

until Rosie suggested they begin their journey and started walking, the kids following at her side.

This was a special time in Konfety Kingdom, when the gnomes would unveil their magical new star constellation. There would be a party all afternoon and a fireworks display that evening just before the elves and fairies lit up the constellation and hung it in the night sky for all the world to enjoy.

Jack and Jill were filled with great anticipation at the privilege of attending this enchanted Celestial star-gazing event being held near the waterfall that…

"Chocolate waterfall," interrupted Charlie.

"That spills into the Chocolate Milk River," Maddie quickly added.

"Oh, right!" Mima acknowledged the clarification and made the correction.

…at the chocolate waterfall that spilled into the Chocolate Milk River that flowed between the Fairy Kingdom and the Woodlands of the Gnomes.

As they walked, Rosie kept looking expectantly from side to side, checking behind her, as if she was expecting a troll to suddenly pop out from behind a rock candy boulder.

Jack looked at Jill with questioning eyes and a smile stretched across his face. Jill giggled.

"Who or what are you looking for, Rosie?"

"OH!" *Startled, Rosie turned her head forward. "I keep hearing something, and I can't figure out what it is."*

"I'll bet it's the elves, coming to see Jack and Jill," suggested Charlie.

"No, it's the fairies." Sophi challenged her cousin.

"It can't be the fairies or the elves." Maddie rolled her eyes as if these were absurd suggestions. "They are all busy getting ready for this evening."

"How about having it be the elf and fairy children?" proposed Mima.

The girls all agreed and Mima went on with the tale.

Jack and Jill listened intently but couldn't hear any footsteps or twigs breaking. Not even the rustling of a single blade of licorice grass could be detected swaying in the stillness.

"Let's keep moving." Rosie tossed her long, beautiful mane. "It's probably just my mind working overtime. I'm so excited for tonight's event that my imagination is running wild!"

They were hurrying along the candied cobblestone trail when suddenly Jack heard it too.

"What's that?" Jack stopped so suddenly that Jill bumped into him, nearly knocking him over.

"Ow!" Jill cried out. "Why did you stop? Did you hear something?"

"I heard the sound of a candied stone being kicked."
Jack held his hand to his ear and listened intently.

They all looked around. Still not seeing anyone, they
quickened their pace.

"Who's there?" challenged Jill a few moments later,
twirling around so quickly that she caught sight of
something or someone jumping behind a popcorn ball
bush. "I see you! Come out, come out, whoever you are!"

To their surprise, a boy elf and a girl fairy scampered
out from behind the bush, giggling.

"Ha, ha, ha!" the ornery pair laughed out loud. "We
got you good!"

Relieved that it was just two littles, Rosie and the
children joined in the fun.

"You had us questioning our senses." Rosie snorted.
"Let me introduce you to this playful pair. This is…"

Mima paused, giving the cousins the opportunity to
come up with a name.

"The girl should be Sparkle," Maddie blurted out.

"And the boy should be Milo," added Charlie.

Mima nodded her head and, without skipping a
beat, introduced the two new characters.

"This is Sparkle." Rosie pointed her nose toward the
fairy. "And this is her cohort, Milo."

The elf and the fairy bowed gracefully.

"And you must be Jack and Jill." Milo stood tall as he greeted the children. "We've been dying to meet you ever since Rosie told us how you helped her out of the taffy puddle mess she found herself in." Then, scowling at Rosie, he huffed, "But Rosie won't ever let us tag along."

"Yeah," Sparkle pouted. "Rosie always tells us about your adventures AFTER they happen. We didn't want to be left behind again, so we decided to follow her."

"We weren't going to let her get away this time." Milo planted his hands firmly on his hips.

"You're a couple of sneaky creatures." Jack chuckled in admiration. "Happy to meet you!"

"Me too!" Jill stepped cautiously toward the fairy and inquired, "Do you really have fairy dust that can make people fly?"

"Only special fairies have that magical power," explained Sparkle. "I know of only a few in all the land."

"Wow!" Jill was completely captivated by this new clarification.

"Come along." Rosie looked directly at Milo and Sparkle. "ALL of you! But you two had better be on your best behavior, or I'll think twice before allowing you to join us again!"

Sparkle and Milo didn't waste a single moment. "Yes, Ms. Rosie!" they agreed and jumped onto the candy cobblestone trail to join the rest of the party.

It wasn't long before they came to a fork in the road. If they turned left, they would travel through the land of the elves. Turning right would take them straight to the Fairy Kingdom.

"We should turn left," stated Milo.

"Oh no! We'll go right!" Sparkle boldly demanded.

"Left," Milo countered, raising his voice.

"Right!" Sparkle insisted as she tauntingly fluttered around Milo.

"Have you two so quickly forgotten your promise to behave?" Rosie looked sternly from one to the other.

"They should do rock, paper, scissors to decide which way to go," Sophi eagerly suggested. "That's what Maddie and I do!"

Mima and the girls agreed it was a great idea.

"Let's do rock, paper, scissors," suggested Jack.

"What's that?" Milo wrinkled his forehead in deep confusion.

Jill explained the hand gestures and how the game was played. They all agreed that Jack and Jill would show them how it was done and that whoever won two rounds out of three would get to choose which direction the party went.

"One, two, three," Milo counted, following Jill's instructions. On three, Jack made a rock and Jill made paper.

"Paper covers the rock. That's one!" Jill announced enthusiastically.

Milo began once more, "One, two, three."

Again Jack made the sign for rock, but Jill signed scissors.

"Ha! Ha! Ha! Rock smashes scissors!" Jack exclaimed triumphantly. "One more time, Milo!"

Caught up in the game, Milo eagerly heeded Jack's command.

"One, two, three."

This time, Jack signed paper and Jill did scissors.

"Scissors cut paper! I won!" Jill shouted as she jumped up and down. "We get to go by way of the Fairy Kingdom!"

"Dang!" Jack snarled as he stomped his foot.

Rosie gave Jack a look that made them all laugh, for they knew how Rosie felt about temper tantrums. No one wanted to see the wrath of Rosie on such a special day, so they all turned right and headed off to the Fairy Kingdom, laughing and joking and having fun.

Before they knew it, they were crossing the toffee bridge sprinkled with nuts, that led to the Kingdom.

"I'm hungry," Jack announced as they crossed the bridge.

"Here you go." Sparkle broke off a piece of toffee and handed some to both Jack and Jill.

"Mmm! Yummy!" Jack munched loudly on his toffee.

"This is so de-licious!" agreed Jill. "And I'll never get used to the amazing fact that whatever you take always replenishes itself.

"You're so lucky!" Jack reached for another chunk of the sweet candy. "You never run out of these incredible, tasty treats!"

"If you think this is good, you should see all the food they have prepared for the banquet." Sparkle pointed ahead to rows and rows of long tables filled with platters and bowls of scrumptious food.

"Oh my!" Jill's eyes twinkled with delight. "Look at that waterfall, or should I say 'chocolate fall,' and all that food, and…" Her voice trailed off.

Jack could hardly believe his eyes! They had been to Konfety Kingdom many times before, but he had never seen a celebration like this.

The sun was rising high in the sky, and the group was hot and thirsty. As beads of sweat began forming on their faces, they each picked a sugar-cookie-shaped flower and, after eating the petals, used the stems as straws to drink the chocolate milk that flowed nearby.

"Ah…" Milo smacked his lips as he lay back on the licorice grass and folded his hands behind his head.

Jack mimicked Milo and soon all four of them were talking and bantering about this, that, and the other.

After a few moments of relaxation, Rosie gathered the crew and they went to explore the celebration. Jack and Jill knew many of the magical creatures from previous adventures. The creatures all welcomed the pint-sized humans and showed them around. There were games to play and food to eat, and new friends to make, as well as music and dancing.

"Hey Mima!" Sophi tapped on Mima's lap. "When do they get to see the stars?"

"Can I tell the part where they get the new constellation?" Charlie batted her big brown eyes, pleading for the opportunity to create her part of the story.

"I think that's a great idea, Charlie!" Mima looked over at her youngest granddaughter. "And Sophi can make the sun go down."

"Can I do the ending?" requested Maddie.

They all agreed it was a great plan, and Sophi began.

Eventually, the sun began to set behind the ice cream mountains and the moon was bright in the sky. Now, it was time for the fireworks. Jack and Jill could hardly wait!

Bang! Boom! The fireworks sprayed their colorful magic sprinkles across the sky.

Jack and Jill had never seen fireworks quite like this before. They were stunningly beautiful.

"Stunningly, huh?" Mima wondered with a chuckle. "That's a pretty big word for you!"

Sophi grinned proudly.

"My turn," Charlie announced and immediately began to add her part.

As soon as the fireworks were over, a big fluffy cotton candy cloud appeared before their eyes. Fairies danced around and elves scurried about, getting into place.

Then the great Woodland Gnome King stepped up to the microphone. "It's been a long time since a new star has been introduced into this part of the sky," he boomed. "Tonight, we celebrate our great neighbors to the north."

The fairies continued to dance excitedly above the stage, flitting and fluttering about.

"I have asked several of the fairies and elves to help us hang this new set of stars." And with a wave of the mighty gnome's hand, the cotton candy clouds lifted and revealed a constellation in the shape of the Fairy Princess with her wand held high, spreading magic to all below.

"Oh! That's cool, Charlie," congratulated Maddie. "Can I take over now?"

Charlie waved her hand, as if passing the fairy wand to Maddie. The girls all giggled, and then Maddie took over.

Cheers went up all around and the Fairy Princess blushed so brightly, her smile sparked the last of the fireworks, which lit up the stars in the new constellation.

There was much dancing and clapping and celebrating all the night through. Jack and Jill stayed the night in Rosie's barn with her baby unicorn Petunia. The next morning, they made their way back to the east entrance of Konfety Kingdom with Petunia, Sparkle, and Milo all tagging along.

"This has been such great fun!" Jack shook Milo's hand. "I am sad it's over."

"Me too!" Jill nuzzled Petunia one last time. "But we promise to come back soon!"

"Yay!" Sparkle and Milo high-fived each other.

Rosie whinnied softly as she gently nudged Jack and Jill onto the gumdrop trail.

"Until we meet again, my friends, keep your eye on the sky and know that the Fairy Princess is watching over you."

"The End!" Maddie smiled, pleased with her ending.

"That was a good story." Sophi sighed sleepily.

They all agreed it was one of their best stories yet as they crawled into their sleeping bags.

Mima tip-toed silently out of the tent and over to Papa who stirred the last of the dying embers, a smirk spread across his face, exactly as she had imagined.

He patted the chair next to him.

"Good job, Mima," he said quietly as they snuggled and gazed up at the star-filled sky. "I wonder what the Fairy Princess would have to say about your story?" He glanced over at Mima's happy face and winked.

Playful Preparation

At breakfast the next morning, the girls were still talking about the Konfety Kingdom adventure.

"We should do some star-gazing this evening and see if we can find the new Fairy Princess constellation." Charlie smiled at Maddie and Sophi from across the table.

"Maybe it's hanging next to the North Star." Sophi's eyes twinkled.

"Oh! Oh!" Maddie started excitedly. "Maybe the tip of the Fairy Princess's wand can be the North Star!"

"You ladies have amazing imaginations." Papa grabbed a few blueberries and popped them into his mouth one by one.

"Those, my dear, are for breakfast," Mima scolded playfully.

Papa looked offended, using his big brown eyes to his advantage to look extra heartbroken.

"You're impossible!" Mima tossed him a towel. "Maybe you could bring the pot of oatmeal to the table while the girls gather the bowls and spoons."

Smiling, Papa fetched the porridge and began filling their bowls.

"Mmm! Break-fast! Break-fast!" Sophi chanted.

Maddie and Charlie joined in and added the thump thump of their spoons hitting the table in **cadence** with the chant.

Exasperated, Mima threw her hands up in the air and rolled her eyes at them all in mock disgust.

"I give up! You're all on my ornery list today! I think we might have to double the hike to work off all of this extra energy everyone seems to have."

"Not a longer hike," Charlie moaned.

To encourage Mima, Maddie changed the words and began chanting, "Hike! Hike! Hike!"

"Oh my heavens!" Mima laughed and collapsed onto the bench next to Sophi. "It's like a three-ring circus around here!"

Everyone joked and giggled all through breakfast.

With bellies full for the moment, they were ready to start their hike, but there were a few chores to do before they could be on their way.

"You girls gather up your backpacks, hats, and jackets while Papa and I clean up the dishes."

"What?" squealed Papa, a grin spreading across his face. "I have to help clean up this mess?"

"You helped make it." Charlie smirked.

"It's your turn, Papa!" Maddie shook her finger scoldingly.

"Papa has to do dishes!" Sophi sang.

"Oh, you think so?" Papa put his hands on his hips and pouted. "What if I don't wanna?"

"You're funny! I'll bet Mima won't give you any snacks if you don't shape up," Charlie warned.

"Come on, Papa," coaxed Mima. "You wouldn't want to lose your snacks!"

"Not the snacks, Papa!" Sophi cautioned. "You can lose anything else, but NOT the snacks!"

"Sophi's right." Mima winked at Sophi. "We'll be mixing up a special trail mix concoction and you don't want to be left out of that!"

Papa shrugged his shoulders.

"Dishes it is then," he conceded and began gathering up the dirty bowls and spoons as the girls left the table to prepare their backpacks for the hike.

Mima washed while Papa dried, and soon the camp kitchen was sparkling.

"Are you girls ready to put together your trail mix?" Mima opened up the tote and began unloading her favorite ingredients.

The girls clamored to the table, backpacks in tow. Tossing them into a nearby camp chair, they stood on either side of the table.

"What all goes into trail mix?" Maddie wasn't a big fan of most nuts.

"I hope there are chocolate candies." Sophi smacked her lips.

Mima began setting ingredients out on the table: banana chips, salty peanuts, candy-covered chocolate pieces, cashews, licorice bites, mango chunks, craisins, popcorn, cheesy fish crackers, circle-shaped sugar cereal, and gummy bears.

"Look at all these choices!" A deep furrow formed across Charlie's brow. "How many can we have?"

Chuckling, Papa teased, "You can have one of each." He paused momentarily, then added, "One cracker, one peanut, and one…"

"That's not true, is it, Mima?" Sophi interrupted abruptly.

"Now, Papa…" Mima threw her hands up in the air. "Why do you always have to cause **mayhem** wherever you go?"

"Who, me?" Papa **feigned** ignorance, but his big Cheshire cat grin gave him away,

"Here's how this is going to work," instructed Mima. "You will each get a zipper bag that you can fill with goodies. I don't care how many you take of each item…"

At that precise moment, Papa reached over and grabbed the entire bag of candy-covered chocolates and held them protectively against his chest.

Mima looked sternly at Papa.

"But you have to make sure everyone gets some. That includes you, Papa!"

"Ooh, Papa's in trouble!" Maddie giggled, setting in motion another round of laughter.

Papa winked and **reluctantly** put the candies back, and everyone began filling a bag with their favorite items.

Mima zipped her bag shut.

"Does anyone know what we called trail mix when I was a kid?"

"Uhm… granola?" proposed Charlie.

"Peanut mix," Sophi suggested.

"I'm stumped," replied Maddie.

"Ohh… those are some good guesses and you were pretty close, Sophi. Actually we called it GORP, which stood for Good Old Raisins and Peanuts." Mima laughed. "I find this funny because I didn't like raisins back then, and I am positive that mine always had way more yummy goodness than just raisins and peanuts!"

"That's funny!" Sophi giggled.

"Yuck! I wouldn't like GORP if it was just peanuts and raisins." A grimace formed on Maddie's face.

"What's wrong with peanuts?" Papa reached into the bag of peanuts, pulled out a couple, and popped them into his mouth. "I like peanuts!"

"I like peanuts too, Papa, but just peanuts and raisins?" Charlie paused to find the right words. "That would be so bo-ring!"

Maddie wrinkled up her nose.

"I'll take this trail mix over peanuts anytime!"

They continued chatting as they finished making their own special mixes.

"Alright, girls. Put the trail mix into your backpack, fill up your water bottles, and then we'll talk about the scavenger hunt."

When everyone was ready, they joined Mima at the table.

"Before we start our hike, let's go over the rules of the scavenger hunt." Mima held up a set of cards. "I've laminated pictures of a variety of objects, flowers, insects, and animals that we might find on the trail today.

"Is there a picture of a snake?" Maddie sneaked a peak at her sister.

"Silly girl," chided Mima. "Of course there's a picture of a snake." Her eyes twinkled with anticipation at the response, knowing everyone was likely remembering the last hike with Sophi.

"Oh no!" Sophi exclaimed. "No snakes for me!"

They laughed good-naturedly as Mima continued, "I separated out the pictures so no one set is completely like another. There are similarities, but just like a Bingo card, none are exactly the same."

"I want the set without a snake." Charlie flipped through a set of cards.

"What makes you think there isn't a snake on each of the rings?" Mima smirked.

The girls all looked at each other until Charlie gave voice to their collective thoughts, "I think you've been hanging around Papa too long. He's starting to rub off on you!"

Laughter broke out among the girls as Mima and Papa stared questioningly at each other.

Turning her attention to the three giggling girls, Mima insisted, "There's no way I'm as ornery as Papa!"

Papa shrugged his shoulders, dismissing the accusation, and the girls continued to giggle.

Without skipping a beat, Mima brought the conversation back to the scavenger hunt.

"As you can see, I have punched holes in these photos and attached them to a single keyring so you can easily flip through them as you hike, without losing any of them. Each of you will choose one marker and a set of laminated pictures. When you spot a specific item that matches one of your photos, show it to either Papa or me so we can verify that it's correct. Then, take your marker and draw an X through the picture."

"Does it have to be exactly like the picture?" Maddie reached for a batch of pictures and the blue marker.

"That's a bit tricky," replied Mima. "Some of these photos are of a specific structure, like a sign post. That has to be exactly like the picture. However, if there's a photo of a red 'paintbrush,' a type of flower found in this area, that can be any color as long as the type of flower is the same."

"That makes sense." Charlie picked up the purple marker and a set of pictures.

"What do we get if we find the most pictures?" Sophi chose the pink marker.

"Hmmm…" Mima tapped her chin. "How about whoever wins gets to choose our dessert this evening?"

"Alright!" Sophi shouted. "If I win, I'm choosing s'mores!"

"I would pick playing Chubby Bunnies again." Charlie smiled.

"I think we should make dump cake." Maddie looked up dreamily.

"But what if I win?" Papa questioned.

"I think you get to clean up the mess!" Mima teased.

Papa pretended to sulk, causing everyone to burst out with laughter again.

"On a more serious note…" Mima tried to rally the troops. "While we are searching for all of these pictures, we must stay on the trail. Does anyone know why that's important?"

"There might be snakes like the one we saw last year hiking up to the falls!" offered Charlie.

"Ohhh!" Sophi shuddered. "I remember that snake!"

"I'll never forget how Sophi literally climbed up Mima's leg because she was so scared." Maddie giggled.

"It's not funny!" Sophi pouted.

"Well, actually… " Charlie started to comment but Mima interrupted.

"Okay, girls," cautioned Mima. "While that was humorous to the rest of us, poor Sophi was sincerely scared. That choke hold she had around my neck was no joke! I could barely breathe!"

"Mima!" Sophi grumbled, looking embarrassed.

"Oh, Sophi." Mima moved closer and put a loving arm around her granddaughter. "It's okay to be afraid. We're all afraid of something, at some time. It's what we do with what we learn from the experience that can help us move past our fears."

"What's something that you learned from that experience?" Papa inquired.

"Umm…" Sophi reflected for a moment. "I remember that the snake stayed where it was because we stayed away from it."

"Exactly! What else?" Mima encouraged.

"I remember we talked about how not all snakes have rattles," Sophi added.

"That's right!" Charlie jumped in. "We need to listen while we're hiking. Sometimes the only warning we have is the hissing sound they make."

"Or seeing them slither away as we come around the bend or up over a hill," Sophi interjected.

"We also learned how to tell the difference between a venomous snake and one that's not," recalled Maddie.

"Good job, ladies!" Mima cheered. "Do you remember the difference between the two, Maddie?"

Maddie sat quietly for a moment.

"I think they have different sized heads and eyes, but I can't remember for sure."

"That's correct!" Papa congratulated her. "Non-venomous snakes have rounded or blunt heads and round eyes. Venomous snakes, however, will usually have more of a pointed snout and triangular-shaped head. Their eyes are more of a slit or elliptical shape. This allows them to block out more of the sunlight and see their prey easier in bright light."

"Exactly!" Mima agreed. "There's also the shape of the body to consider. Non-venomous snakes are usually more slender, while a venomous snake's body will be thicker or heavier looking."

"Oh! I remember one more thing," whooped Charlie. "Aren't their tails pointier if they are non-venomous?"

"Yes!" Papa and Mima confirmed.

Papa clarified, "The venomous snakes usually have a rattle or cluster of scales that never taper into a point."

"Is that true for baby snakes?" Maddie questioned. "Excellent question. Baby snakes haven't yet formed their 'rattles' or clusters of scales. Therefore, their tails will look more pointy."

"And aren't the baby snakes more venomous?" Charlie asked.

"Well…" Papa paused momentarily. "While it's true that baby snakes have not yet learned how to control the venom in their bite, adult snakes have a greater quantity of venom."

"Goodness!" Sophi sighed. "There sure is a lot to remember!"

"There are many ways to recognize snakes." Mima took a deep breath. "The important thing to remember is that usually snakes are more afraid of you than you are of them. When seeing a snake, you should immediately stop walking, swinging your arms, and making noise. Back up slowly and wait to see if it's going to quietly slither off the trail and away from you. If it's curled up and hissing, you need to go back the way you came. Live to hike another day or find a different trail."

"Never throw things like rocks or sticks at them," Maddie inserted proudly.

"And never make sudden movements," added Sophi.

"Like climbing up Mima's leg," Charlie snickered. Sophi hissed at Charlie like she was the snake, adding a glaring sideways stare for effect.

"Sounds like you ladies are well-educated in snakes," Papa attempted to distract. "Anything else we should remember while we're out hiking?"

The girls looked questioningly at each other.

"I'll give you a hint." Mima pointed toward their packs. "You each have one in your backpack."

"Snacks!" Sophi exclaimed proudly.

"That's definitely important," acknowledged Mima. "But that was not what I was thinking of. Is there something else in your pack that you should never go hiking without?"

"A water bottle?" Maddie and Charlie guessed in unison.

"Correct!"

Maddie and Charlie gave each other a high-five.

"Everyone take a quick peek at the pictures of the items you'll be searching for." Mima suggested as she picked up her backpack and tossed it onto her shoulders. "Let's head out!"

Maddie glanced through the photos.

"I already found one!"

"That's not fair!" Charlie groaned.

"Hold up!" Mima held up her hand in warning. "The scavenger hunt doesn't start until we get to the trail."

"Sorry, Maddie." Papa glanced at Mima to see if she was paying attention. "If it were up to me, I'd let you have it, but you know what a stickler Mima is with her rules."

"You had better watch out, Papa!" Mima countered, shaking a finger playfully at him.

Sophi slipped her hand into Mima's.

"Looks like Papa's just asking for trouble today, huh Mima?"

Mima squeezed the little one's hand in agreement and smiled as they all walked briskly out of the campsite and up the road to the trailhead.

Papa's smile grew bigger and brighter as he took his place at the back of the pack.

"Tee hee hee..." Papa chuckled to himself, as he tapped his fingers together, indicating that he was plotting and planning what other mischief he might be able to get into along the trail.

Scavenger Surprises

It wasn't long before Sophi was asking for a break and a snack. They all paused on the trail while she plopped down on a log near the edge.

"Look, Papa! A spider! That's one of my cards!"

Papa verified it was indeed one of her items to find, and she excitedly put an X through the photo.

"That's one for me!"

The other two took the opportunity to search a little more closely at their surroundings. Soon Maddie had found a sunflower, its bright yellow petals and burnt orange center creating a brilliant contrast against the tall green grass as well as a wild raspberry bush popping with fruit.

"It even has raspberries on the bush!" Maddie pointed at the dark red berries.

"Can we eat them?" Charlie moved closer to investigate.

"You have to be very careful about the types of berries you eat in the forest. If they have blue, black, or purple skin, there's a good chance they are edible. If the skin is green, white, or yellow or if they grow in bunches, that is a strong indication you should stay away from them. Berries that are red or orange are questionable." Mima paused to make sure the girls were still listening. "Raspberries and mulberries are made of tiny clusters packed together. They will appear to be bumpy. These clusters make them okay to eat. However, you should never just try any berries without someone who knows the difference."

"So…" Sophi tentatively began. "Does that mean we can eat them?

"I happen to know that these are indeed wild raspberries," instructed Mima. "And, because they are dark red and easily pull off of their stem, they are ripe and ready to eat."

"Hurray!" shouted the girls as they all leapt toward the bush.

"You may each pick two."

"We don't want to eat them all or the bears might come after us!" teased Papa, looking around to make sure no bears were in sight.

The girls pretended to ignore him as they picked their berries and enjoyed the sweet juices.

"What's rustling over there?" Papa pointed to a bush several feet off the trail.

The bush was actually moving, and the girls all quickly hid their berry stained hands behind their backs and gawked at the bush.

"It really is moving," announced Sophi nervously.

"I'll bet there's a bear in that bush!" Papa schemed.

"Oh my goodness!" Maddie was startled by something running out from under the bush and up a nearby tree.

"It's a squirrel!" Charlie jumped up and down excitedly, realizing it was one of her items. "Check it out, Papa! Squirrels are one of my cards!" She hurriedly flipped through the cards, found the squirrel, and began waving the card for Papa to certify.

"That was a close one," taunted Papa, attempting to keep the **farce** going while giving Charlie a thumbs-up to check off her card.

"Oh, Papa!" Maddie furrowed her brow. "You're such a joker!"

"Do I wear a pointy jester's hat, with bells on it, and jump around?" Papa inquired with a sneer.

They all laughed at the image Papa had conjured.

Mima held her belly in an attempt to stifle her laugh.

"I'm pretty sure I saw you wearing your pointy hat just last week!"

Everyone burst out in giggles all over again.

"There won't be any bears around here," stated Charlie.

"Why's that?" Sophi asked as she stepped up on a rock.

"Because we're all making way too much noise!" Charlie emphasized.

"We don't need bear bells on this hike," added Maddie. "With Papa along, he'll keep us laughing and making too much noise!"

"We'll for sure scare the bears away," laughed Sophi. "I just wish that worked for snakes!"

They continued on their way, singing songs and laughing at Papa's antics, stopping here and there for a drink of water and a handful of trail mix or to mark off one of their scavenger hunt items.

Over halfway through the hike, Mima and the girls stared intently at the crop of beautiful Colorado Columbines Charlie found.

"Did you know the Columbine is the Colorado state flower?" Mima asked.

Before the girls could acknowledge her words, they heard something stirring loudly just a short way down the path. Branches were swinging back and forth, and a growl came from inside the bush.

The girls all screamed and turned to run as Papa jumped out from behind the bush.

Her heart beating loudly in her ears, Mima managed to grab the tail of Sophi's shirt just before she escaped, then hollered for the other two to come back.

"It's just Papa!" she growled, glaring a warning at Papa as he popped out of the bush grinning from ear to ear.

"You should've seen the looks on your faces!" Papa roared. "I totally had you going!"

"Oh Papa!" Mima shook her head. "You got us good!"

"Mean ol' Papa!" Sophi growled.

"You scared me half to death!" Maddie grumbled as she tried to catch her breath.

"My heart is still racing!" Charlie moaned.

"I think you may have outdone yourself, Papa! You have just won yourself a spot at the front of the line!" Mima motioned for him to take his new position.

"Yeah!" agreed Maddie. "That way we can keep an eye on you!"

"For sure!" affirmed Charlie.

Giving Papa a hostile stare, Sophi added, "That wasn't very nice, Papa!"

"I have lost my cards," Charlie announced sadly. "And my marker too!"

"I'm sorry," said Papa. "I'll help you look for them."

"I saw you throw them when Papa growled." Maddie looked over her shoulder. "I bet they are near the Columbines Mima was telling us about before we were so rudely interrupted." Giving Papa another annoyed look, she wrapped her arms protectively around Charlie and headed in the direction of the flowers a short distance away.

Sadness crept across Papa's brow as they went off without him.

"How do you feel about being a bear now?" Mima questioned.

He looked sorrowfully at Mima.

"I didn't mean to scare them so badly."

"They are still kids." Mima softly reminded him as she took his hand in hers.

"Yeah," mimicked Sophi more emphatically. "We're still kids, Papa!"

Mima and Papa glanced at each other. Papa's sorrow was quickly replaced by a grin as both tried not to laugh out loud.

"You tell him, Sophi," Charlie encouraged her cousin. "You're lucky the little boys aren't here! They'd still be crying."

"Here they are!" Maddie excitedly rescued the cards.

A few moments later, Charlie held up the marker that had flown several feet away near a group of moss covered rocks.

"I found it!"

"Yay!" they all cheered.

"I'm starving!" Sophi held up her empty trail mix bag.

Glancing at the sun high in the sky, Mima nudged Papa to the front of the pack.

"Lead us back to camp, Papa. We have hungry girls to feed!"

"But what if I go the wrong way?"

"Don't try to fool us, Papa," demanded Maddie.

"Mima won't let you go the wrong way," Charlie stated confidently as she fell into line.

Having lost this battle, Papa shrugged his shoulders, letting them all know he would behave… for the moment.

"Do I get to eat too?" Papa patted his belly.

The cousins looked at each other and then back at him.

"What do you say?" Sophi put her hands on her hips for emphasis.

Papa pretended to be thinking hard, then acting as if he had suddenly figured out the answer. "I'm sorry, girls."

"Papa… I forgive you." Sophi gave him a big hug, smiled up at him, and slipped her small hand into his.

Laughing, Papa squeezed her hand lovingly as they headed along the trail toward camp.

After several more stops to investigate a treasure, they turned the corner bringing the campsite into view.

"I didn't think we would ever get back." Sophi sighed wearily. "My tummy is grumbling like Papa's scary bear growl!"

"What's for lunch?" Maddie dropped her backpack onto the table before flopping into her chair.

"How about a peanut butter and jelly sandwich? Would that help curb the rumbly grumblies?"

Maddie wrinkled up her nose, but kept silent as Charlie and Sophi did a happy dance around the picnic table.

Knowing peanut butter wasn't one of Maddie's favorites, Mima put an arm around her and whispered, "Are you okay with a peanut butter sandwich?"

Maddie shrugged her shoulders.

"It's okay, but… could I have mine on a tortilla instead of bread?"

"Absolutely, Maddie." Mima responded with a gentle squeeze to Maddie's shoulders. "And thank you for being so willing to eat it, even though it's not what you'd prefer."

Maddie beamed brightly at the reminder that Mima knew their favorite and not-so-favorite foods, and tried to give them options, when she could.

"Thank you, Mima."

Having finished their dance around the table, Sophi chirped, "What else, what else, what else do we get?!"

"Be patient, little one. I promise we have enough food to fill you up from your toes to the tip of your nose, and then some!"

"Oh yeah," Papa chuckled. "I know how Mima gets when she's **hangry**, so I made sure she packed plenty of food!"

Smiling at Papa knowingly, Mima motioned with her hand for the girls to follow as she headed to the makeshift kitchen to gather all the ingredients needed to make their lunch.

Pinky Promises

Sophi moaned as she finished her last bite, jelly dripping down her chin.

"That was yummmmmmy!"

"I'm so glad you enjoyed it." Mima caught Maddie's eyes and gave her a silent wink as she quickly reached for a washcloth and began wiping off the food that had missed Sophi's mouth and landed on her sweet face.

"What are we going to do now?" Charlie wondered.

"I don't know about you, but I'm ready for a nap," Papa snickered.

Sophi immediately spouted off, "We're too big for naps, Papa!"

"But I'm big, and I still want a nap!"

"Well maybe, if you hadn't used so much of your energy trying to scare us to death," Maddie lectured, "you wouldn't be so tired!"

Sophi and Charlie jumped on the **bandwagon** supporting Maddie's **hypothesis**.

Charlie joined in eagerly, "Yeah! That was so mean, Papa!"

"SO MEAN!" Sophi emphasized.

Papa gave them his saddest puppy-eyes and hung his head. Then, before the girls could even say anything, he announced, "I'm sorry…" and paused before announcing bravely, "But I sure got you good!"

"Get him!" Charlie cried as all three leapt from their seats and chased after him.

Papa ran for a tree, trying to put something between him and the cousins, but Maddie went one way and Charlie another, while Sophi ran directly for Papa.

He swerved this way and that, avoiding the girls momentarily. Soon Maddie's soccer training kicked in and as Papa attempted to swerve on his two bad knees, she countered and caught hold of his shirt.

"We've got you now!" Charlie reached for Papa's arm to keep him from getting away.

"Hold on!" Sophi ran as fast as her legs would carry her toward the trio. "I'm coming!"

Papa was no match for the girls.

"I give up! You win!" He dropped to the soft, grassy ground, bringing the three of them tumbling down with him, but they were not satisfied that Papa had fully paid his dues.

"Tickle him!" shouted Sophi, leaping from nearby.

The other two followed Sophi's war cry and they all tackled Papa and began tickling him mercilessly.

Papa tried to roll away, but the girls were determined to make him pay for his antics and lack of **remorse.**

"Help me, Mima!" Papa bellowed amidst whoops and hollers from the girls.

"Looks like you're getting just what you deserve," Mima scolded, grateful it was Papa and not her in trouble with these high-spirited young ladies.

"Are you sorry, yet?" Charlie looked Papa straight in the eyes.

"And we mean REALLY sorry!" Maddie emphasized.

"Yeah, no pretending!" Sophi stood in a superhero pose, arms on hips.

Gasping for breath, Papa confessed that he was truly sorry for scaring them. However, the grin he was trying to stifle didn't match his words, and the girls knew how much Papa loved to tease them.

"Pinky promise you'll never scare us like that again, Papa." Charlie held out her pinky for him to promise.

"Us too!" Maddie and Sophi added their pinkies to the lineup.

"What? I have to pinky promise?" Papa let out a deep, long sigh.

"Yes!"

"Hmm…" Mima snickered as she walked toward Papa. "Sounds like they are going to hold you to your word! Looks like you've got yourself into quite the pickle!"

Papa glanced in her direction.

"You're really not going to help a guy out, are you?"

"Nope," Mima responded firmly. "You took this one a little too far, so we girls have to stick together this time!"

Seeing that he was not going to win this battle, Papa finally conceded and pinky promised with each of the cousins.

As soon as they were finished, the girls all helped Papa to his feet. Feeling proud of themselves, they strutted back to the table where Mima had put a container full of games and some leftover chocolate chip cookies.

"Anybody want to play cards with me?"

"I will, if I can have a cookie," quipped Sophi.

"Mmmm… cookies!" Charlie murmured softly.

"Cards and cookies sounds like fun, but I want to know who won the scavenger hunt." Maddie's eyes glimmered with confidence.

"Oh, heavens! How did I forget that part? There must have been a distraction!" Mima gave Papa a final chastising side glance. "Let's figure that out right now. Bring me your stacks of cards and we'll count them."

The girls eagerly ran to gather their cards from the pile of backpacks scattered on the ground.

"You've got my cards, Sophi," Maddie snapped. "See, they have the blue marker on them!"

"I was just going to hand them to you," Sophi whined with frustration.

"Where are my cards?" Charlie pushed the packs around with her foot.

"Why don't you lean over and pick those packs up," Mima suggested. "Work together. Help each other out."

Finding all three stacks of cards, the girls ran back to Mima.

"Count mine first!" Sophi waved her cards in the air.

Mima looked at Sophi sternly.

"Excuse me. I think you're forgetting something."

Sophi paused briefly and then squealed, "Please!"

"That's a magical word." A big grin spread across Mima's face as she reached for Sophi's cards. "Let's see how many you found."

They counted up Sophi's cards together.

"One, two, three… ten, eleven, and twelve," they said as Mima placed the last marked card on the pile.

"Nicely done!" congratulated Mima.

"Mine next!" Charlie excitedly held up her cards. Then remembering Mima's **admonition**, she added, "Please!"

Charlie's count went even higher.

"Twelve, thirteen, fourteen!"

"I have fourteen! Oh, I hope I win!" Charlie jumped up and down in her seat. "I want to play Chubby Bunnies again!"

"Grrr…" Sophi stomped her foot on the ground. "I wanted s'mores!"

Maddie had been patiently waiting, but couldn't resist challenging Charlie.

"I hope I win! Then we can have dump cake!"

Mima gave all three girls a thoughtful glance.

"We'll have a yummy dessert, no matter who wins."

"True." Charlie sighed. "But we had so much fun playing Chubby Bunnies!"

"Yeah." A grin spread across Maddie's face. "Sophi nearly spit hers out on the table!"

"And I almost lost mine too!" Charlie joined in the laughter.

"We were all a sight," agreed Mima. "Let's count Maddie's cards so we know what to plan for dessert."

"One, two, three…" they began counting. Maddie was intent on the cards, watching each one for a big blue X."

"Nine, ten, eleven…" The count continued.

Charlie fidgeted in her seat.

"Ohh! It's going to be close!"

"Thirteen, fourteen…"

Mima held the last card upside-down in her hand, creating an extra portion of suspense.

"Come on, Mima!" the girls clamored.

Mima looked at them as they all stared at the card in her hand. Flipping it over slowly, she revealed a bright blue X on the card.

"Fifteen!" shouted Maddie.

"Good job, Maddie." Charlie congratulated her cousin.

"Thanks, Charlie!" Maddie grinned. "Maybe Mima will let us help her make it!"

"Absolutely! I would love your help. Now, who wants to beat me in a game of cards?"

"I will!" Papa jumped up and grabbed the seat across from Mima.

The girls filled in on both sides of the table as Mima shuffled the Uno cards and Charlie passed the cookies.

They played games for a couple hours, taking turns winning and losing, giggling and teasing each other. As the sun began making its way down the western sky, Papa laid down his last card and with a sly smile declared, "Looks like I won this one!"

"Oh, Papa!" Sophi tossed down her last few cards.

"Ohhh... I was so close. I only had one card left." Charlie laid down her final card, showing a blue zero.

"At least you don't have a gazillion points in your hand," Maddie teasingly complained as she laid down her handful of cards in a rainbow of colors and numbers.

"Yes, but I had two wild cards that I was all ready to lay down." Mima set her cards out for all to see. "And those are worth more points than all the cards in your hand."

Maddie giggled.

"I am so glad we were able to come on this trip!"

"It's been so much fun," agreed Charlie.

"And we've had some yummy food!" Sophi tried playfully to wink at Mima.

"Hmm…" Mima pretended to be pondering Sophi's wink. "Does this mean someone is getting hungry?"

"Yes… yes… YES!" cheered Sophi.

Papa stood up and stretched. "Must be time for me to get a fire going. Who wants to help me?"

Sophi jumped up excitedly.

"I'll help you, Papa!" She ran to catch up with him, reaching for his outstretched hand.

Her small hand slipped comfortably into his, and the two of them set off looking for kindling to start the fire.

"Shall we make dinner and dump cake?" Mima cast her eyes to the two girls at the table.

Maddie and Charlie eagerly agreed and began putting away all the cards and wiping up the cookie crumbs, making room to prepare the next delicious meal.

"When you're finished putting things away, meet me in the kitchen."

They hurriedly put the games back in the tote, snapped the lid on, and scurried after Mima.

Kitchen Elves

"Tonight, we're going to do some dutch oven cooking." Mima pulled out two large cast iron cooking pots and handed one to each of the girls as she motioned for them to place the objects on the table they had just cleared.

The girls looked at each other curiously as they wrapped their arms around them.

"Wow! These are heavy." Charlie breathed heavily as she and Maddie lugged their weighty loads to the table and set them down with a thud.

The girls turned around just in time to see Mima hanging tight to a bag of potatoes along with the box of supplies.

Maddie dashed toward her, grabbing the potatoes just before they landed on the ground.

"Whew!" Maddie gasped triumphantly.

"Nice catch, Maddie!" congratulated Mima.

"Good thing you're so fast, Maddie," Charlie cheered as she relieved Mima of her box of goodies.

"Maddie, would you grab the other container of items I sat out over there, please." Mima pointed toward the box just inside the tent.

Peering into the container, Charlie appeared to recognize the ingredients.

"Is this for the dump cake?"

"I think the cake mix and peaches gave it away," Maddie chimed in, setting down her load and examining the box Charlie had brought over.

The girls giggled at their detective skills.

"Okay, you two." Mima chuckled at how easily they had arrived at the correct answer. "Let's get supper ready first. Then, we'll prepare dessert so it can cook while we eat."

Turning toward the fire pit, Mima could see the pile of small sticks, pine needles, and dried leaves Sophi and Papa had gathered and were attempting to light.

"How's that fire coming? Looks like you have quite the pile of kindling there!"

"You can never have too much kindling, Mima," stated Sophi confidently.

"She is quite the fire builder," Papa acknowledged as the first flames caught hold and began to devour the kindling.

"This is going to be a great fire!" The littlest cousin beamed proudly.

Turning back to the older girls to finish the task at hand, Mima began unloading the contents of the first box.

"What exactly are we making for dinner?" Charlie wondered out loud.

"And what's dutch oven cooking?" asked Maddie.

"Those heavy pots are called dutch ovens. Back when your great-great-great-grandmother cooked over an open fire, these pots were used every day," explained Mima. "Also, these cast iron pots have to be seasoned and cleaned in a special way to keep them from rusting."

"Sounds like a lot of work," Maddie said decidedly.

"I'm sure it was," Mima agreed. "Now, since you two are such great detectives, what do you think we should make with all these ingredients?"

"Well..." Charlie reflected momentarily and then began to list the ingredients. "We have flour, salt, onions, carrots, potatoes, meat chunks, and baking powder.

"Dad uses some of these ingredients when he cooks a roast, except..." Maddie paused. "I don't remember him using flour, baking powder, or salt."

"Yeah, and these are beef chunks, not a roast," added Charlie.

Mima waited patiently as the girls worked toward a conclusion.

Suddenly Maddie's face lit up.

"What if it's more than one dish, Charlie?"

Charlie's eyes brightened as she turned to Mima.

"Are you trying to trick us, Mima?"

"Who, me?" Mima pretended to be shocked. "That's Papa's job."

Both girls rolled their eyes at Mima, knowing she was the **culprit** this time.

"I'll bet you're right, Maddie, but what could the other items be for?"

"Hmm..." Maddie had been contemplating this very question.

The girls took a few more moments, talking among themselves before Mima interjected, "Any final guesses? We need to get this dinner prepared or it will be midnight before we eat."

Maddie and Charlie had huddled together, whispering and debating the possibilities.

"Oh, NO!" Sophi had left the fire-tending to Papa and overheard Mima's warning. "I'll starve by then!"

Mima tugged affectionately on Sophi's ponytails.

"We'll definitely eat before midnight." She turned back to the other two and requested their attention. "A roast was close, but not correct, and how about those extra ingredients?"

"Okay," started Charlie. "We think it's..." she glanced at Maddie for confirmation.

Maddie nodded her head at Charlie and the two answered with anticipation, "We think it's stew and biscuits!"

"Oh! I hope so! I love me some campfire stew and biscuits," Papa added as he joined the ladies.

"That was some super **sleuthing**. Yes," Mima confirmed, "we're having campfire stew."

"What about the biscuits?" asked Sophi.

"It was a good guess, but I think you will like my Indian Fry Bread even better."

"Ohh! Fry bread!" Maddie and Charlie jumped up and down excitedly.

"What's fry bread?" Sophi asked, turning up her nose.

"It's like a sopapilla," explained Mima. "I think you're going to love them!"

"Oh yeah!" Papa smacked his lips at the idea of the yummy goodness. "You can put butter and honey on them, and they are SO yummy!"

"Let's get cooking." Maddie was anxious to learn how to make the meal.

"Sophi and I will go check on the fire." Papa knew that too many cooks in the kitchen was a recipe for disaster.

"Do we need a big fire?" Sophi asked Mima.

"What we really need," began Mima, handing over a mysterious bag to Papa, "is a good bed of hot coals and some charcoal."

"Come on, Sophi." Papa hefted the bag over his shoulder. "We'll let the girls prepare dinner, and I'll show you what to do with these." He shook the bag playfully.

"What's in there, Papa?" Sophi was close on his heels.

"Charcoal. This is how we'll create the heat needed to cook our dinner. We could do it with wood, but it's harder to **regulate** the temperature."

They knelt next to the firepit, and Papa carefully opened the bag to show Sophi the black coal squares.

"These squares are called briquettes and are really, really messy, so we have to be careful not to get it all over our hands." Papa opened the bag wide so Sophi could peek inside. "You can help me pour out a pile of them onto this bed of embers our fire has created."

Sophi followed his lead.

"But won't these catch on fire if we put them here? Like when I roasted my marshmallow and it went up in flames?"

"They will catch on fire, but they are supposed to. We need to watch for them to turn white. That means they're ready to use."

Meanwhile, Maddie and Charlie cleaned all of the vegetables and chopped them into bite-sized chunks while Mima browned the beef chunks. With everyone working together, they had the stew ready to cook in no time.

Papa and Sophi both watched closely as the charcoal finally caught fire and began to turn white around the edges.

Papa turned toward Mima.

"Would you please bring the tongs when you come?"

"Sure, Papa!" Mima picked up the tool.

As they carried their treasure toward the fire, they suddenly heard Papa burst out laughing.

"Oh, Sophi!" Papa gasped. "How did you do that?"

"What...?" Sophi looked confused.

"Your face is as black as your hands." Papa shook his head in disbelief and stared down at the pile of charcoal beside her.

"Uh-oh," sighed Sophi. "I was just gonna move the bag, but some charcoal fell out. I was picking it up, but I forgot you told me not to touch it with my hands."

"No harm done," replied Mima. "Come with me, and I will help you get cleaned up before you get any more charcoal on your clothes."

"But I want to see how to cook the stew," she whined.

"I have an idea, but you have to promise," consoled Mima, "you won't touch anything and I'll grab a rag to clean you up so you can watch Papa work his magic."

"Deal!" Sophi sniffled as she brushed a tear from her eye with her sleeve.

Mima took off for the kitchen and Papa sat seven briquettes in a circle inside the fire pit.

"Each of these coals puts off heat. The trick is to make sure there's just enough heat and that it's spread out evenly."

The girls watched intently as Papa arranged the coals.

"Usually, seven to nine squares on the bottom and five on top will do the trick. We should have it boiling and cooking shortly."

Making sure the lid was secure, he lifted the pot of stew and set it on top of the coals, then added five coals to the top.

"Won't that burn the stew?" Charlie asked, concerned about the dinner they had worked hard to prepare.

"First, that's why we have to be careful about how many coals we place underneath. We don't want it getting too hot. Second, do you see the short nubs on the bottom of the pot?" questioned Papa.

The girls all nodded their heads affirmatively.

"These little feet hold the pot up off the coals so it doesn't burn the bottom."

"Plus," added Mima, arriving back at the fire, "the stew has broth so it's not as likely to scorch and burn as the cake is."

"Wow." Maddie took a deep breath. "There's a lot to learn about dutch oven cooking!"

"Yes, there is," replied Papa. "But once you get the hang of it, magic happens!"

"Like the fairies in our stories!" mused Sophi, face and hands clean once more. "Poof," she announced, swinging a pretend fairy wand over the stew. "It's going to be super yummy now!"

They all laughed as Sophi proudly took a bow.

"Come on, girls. Let's go make the fry bread. With all this magic, the soup will be ready and waiting on us and there will be no bread to go with it."

They all walked away, leaving Papa to tend to the fire and the stew.

"Grab that bowl, Charlie," instructed Mima. "And Maddie, you can gather the measuring cups and spoons. Sophi, will you help me pour some oil into this pan?"

The girls worked together and soon watched as the bread fried in the hot oil.

"This bread smells deeelicciioouus!" exclaimed Sophi.

Mima chuckled.

"Why Sophi, I do believe you're now as white with flour as you were black with coal!"

"I'd rather be covered in flour than dirty ol' coal. It tasted nasty!"

"Yuck!" declared Charlie.

"Gross! Why would you put it in your mouth?" Maddie scrunched up her face.

"I didn't mean to." Sophi quickly defended herself.

"Now, girls," scolded Mima. "I'm sure the flour tastes better than that yucky ol' coal, for sure." She knelt down and once again wiped off Sophi's face.

"Is it time to make the dump cake now?" Maddie was eager to start on her winning dessert.

"Yes, it is." Mima removed the last piece of golden bread from the skillet and onto a paper towel.

The girls all scurried over to the table and Maddie passed out the supplies.

"Sophi gets the butter and Charlie gets the peaches."

"Why do you get to decide?" grumbled Sophi.

"Because she won the contest," Mima reminded her.

Maddie beamed proudly while she took the soda and the cake mix for herself.

"Okay, Mima. I think we're ready!"

"Can I open the peaches?" Charlie was ready, can opener in hand.

"You may," replied Mima. "And Sophi, here's a plastic knife to cut the butter into chunks while Maddie opens up the soda and cake mix."

The girls all followed Mima's instructions and soon were waiting for the next set of directions.

"Okay Charlie, you go first. Dump in the peaches."

They all watched as the sticky goo and peaches slopped into the bottom of the pan.

"Make sure you scrape the can with that spatula next to you, and no licking it," instructed Mima.

"Darn it!" Charlie giggled mischievously. "I was hoping to have a treat!"

"Okay, Maddie. It's your turn. Sprinkle the cake mix evenly over the top of the peaches."

"Yeah, Maddie. Don't dump it all in one spot," Sophi teased as she carefully sliced the butter.

"But I thought it was dump cake," Maddie bantered back as she giggled.

"Okay, you silly girls. Next, we need one cup of soda," directed Mima.

Maddie carefully measured the soda and then asked, "Can I dump this in next?"

"I would pour it around, so you cover as much of the cake as possible," suggested Mima.

"There's nothing left, so it must be my turn?" Sophi guessed hopefully.

"We saved the toughest job for last," Mima teased. "Are you ready?"

"Uh-huh," said Sophi, slicing the last chunk of the butter.

"Take each piece of butter and arrange them on top, making sure they are not all in one area."

"Nice job, Sophi!" Maddie encouraged her little sister. "This cake is going to be scrumpdillyicious!"

Sophi placed the last bit of butter onto the cake.

"Who gets to stir it all together?"

"No one," replied Mima. "That's the magic of it. As it cooks, it mixes together all by itself!"

"Cool." Charlie's tone was one of wonder.

Maddie lifted the lid and put it on top as she whispered, "Don't let Papa see it until it's all cooked."

Mima chuckled at the girls' attempt to pick on Papa.

"You'll have to keep an eye on him, so he doesn't sneak a peek." Mima went along with their joke.

As the ladies all headed toward the fire pit, Charlie called out, "Is the stew ready, Papa?"

Using a special tool called a lid lifter, Papa opened up the kettle of stew. The thick liquid was bubbling and boiling.

"I'm going to need a fork to test the vegetables."

"I'll get it!" called Sophi.

Running quickly toward the picnic table, she grabbed a fork and was just getting ready to run back when Mima interjected, "Walk back with that fork, young lady. I don't want you to trip and hurt yourself."

Obediently, Sophi slowed to a fast walk and handed the utensil to Papa.

Papa poked several potatoes and carrots before announcing, "Stew is ready!"

"Yippee!" the girls shouted as they scurried back to the picnic table.

"Ooh! We need to cook the dump cake," reminded Maddie.

"And no peeking at it, Papa," Charlie warned.

"What? I can't peek?" Papa looked dejectedly toward the fire.

The girls all giggled.

"It's a surprise!" Maddie stifled another laugh.

Mima took the dutch oven filled with its yummy goodness over to the fire pit.

"I better take care of this one," Mima suggested with a wink. "You can help by carrying the stew."

Papa carefully transferred the heavy pot of steaming liquid over to the picnic table while Maddie found a ladle to scoop it and Charlie brought over the fry bread.

"Let's see." Mima looked over the table. "We are missing a couple of important items."

"We have the stew and the fry bread," observed Charlie.

"What else is there?" Maddie looked up and down the table.

"Oh! I know!" Sophi cried out triumphantly. "We need butter and honey for the bread!"

"Good job, Sophi," said Papa. "That's like forgetting the frosting on a cake!"

Sophi beamed proudly as Papa scooped up a bowl for each of them and Mima arrived back at the table with butter and honey in hand.

Once everyone was seated, Papa showed the girls how to bite off a corner of the fry bread and insert the butter and honey into the hole.

"Mmm… This is amazing!" Charlie licked her chin to catch a dribble of honey that was trying to escape. "I love fry bread!"

"Me too!" Maddie took another bite of her bread, butter and honey oozing down her wrist. "But my dump cake is going to be even better!

Sophi finished the last of the stew in her bowl.

"I'm full!"

"What?" Mima joked. "You mean we finally filled you up, from your toes to the tip-top of your head?"

"Yes!" Maddie chuckled slyly. "That means more dump cake for me!"

"Nope!" Sophi declared emphatically. "I have only filled up my dinner stomach. I still have room in my dessert stomach!"

"Oh my goodness!" Papa chuckled. "Sophi, you're full of surprises!"

Mealtime Magic

Remembering it was supposed to be a surprise, Mima sent Papa off to gather firewood for their evening fire while she gathered the girls around the fire pit.

"Are you ready to check on your dump cake?"

The girls stomped their feet excitedly.

"Yes, yes, yes!"

"Can I lift the lid?" asked Maddie hopefully.

"I think I'll do that," replied Mima, "but you can have the first peek at the magic you created."

Kneeling next to the fire pit, careful not to get too close, Maddie was ready as Mima carefully lifted the lid just far enough for her to sneak a glance. The aroma **wafted** out of the dutch oven and swirled into the air.

"Mmm…" Maddie inhaled deeply. "That smells wonderful!"

"Oh, yeah!" agreed Charlie.

"And it looks like little biscuits on top." Maddie smiled proudly.

"Let me see!" cried Sophi.

Mima lifted the lid off so the other two could see inside.

"Wow! It really is like magic!" Maddie marveled. "Look at the way it all mixed together and we didn't stir it a bit."

"Is it ready?" Charlie wondered.

Mima used a toothpick to test the cake, making sure it wasn't doughy.

"Looks good to me!" She placed the cover back on the pot. "Let's just set it off to the side so it can cool for a few minutes while we finish cleaning up dinner."

The girls turned and followed Mima over to the kitchen where they began gathering up the food and rinsing off the dishes, singing silly songs, and not paying any attention to the cake.

Soon Papa returned with an armful of wood and was setting it near the pit when he smelled something yummy and spotted the dutch oven set off to the side.

Maddie, having seen Papa return to camp, decided to tip-toe quietly toward him to make sure he behaved.

Curiosity got the best of him, and Papa reached for the tool to lift the lid.

When she saw that he was up to no good, Maddie moved quiet and quick as a fox closer and closer until she stood only a couple of steps away.

Papa leaned over the pot and was just about to hook the tool onto the lid when Maddie scolded loudly from behind, "What do you think you're doing, Papa?"

Startled, Papa jumped up and flung his arms in the air, letting go of the tool, sending it skyward.

"Watch out!" Maddie hollered as the tool landed itself right in the middle of the fire pit, sending sparks flying. Fortunately, the coals all remained contained in the fire pit.

Mima, Charlie, and Sophi had been watching from the picnic table and saw Maddie scare Papa. Charlie and Sophi were laughing so hard that they fell onto the ground in a fit of giggles while Papa tried to explain his actions.

"I... I... I wwwas just, uhhhhh..." Papa stuttered, staring down at Maddie. Her hands were on her hips and eyes staring up sternly at him. He had been caught in the act and wasn't going to wiggle his way out of this predicament.

"I should ground you, Papa," said Maddie matter-of-factly.

Papa looked over at Mima who just shrugged her shoulders.

"Looks like you've met your match!" She put her hand to her mouth to cover a smile.

Maddie struggled to hold her composure. With the girls on the ground, it was becoming increasingly difficult to not laugh, but she stood firm.

Looking at this mini Mima, he knew it was no good to defend himself. He shouldn't have tried to peek, so he threw up his hands in surrender.

"You're right, Maddie, but I couldn't resist the smell coming from the pot!"

That was it. Maddie couldn't hold it any longer and broke out laughing.

"I scared you good! Just like you did to us, pretending you were a bear!"

Realizing the joke was on him, Papa joined in the laughter.

"You're getting too big for your britches!"

"What are britches?" asked Sophi innocently.

"Britches are pants," explained Mima. "Papa is just realizing that you girls are growing up and he's going to have to be more clever if he's going to keep teasing you."

"Yeah." Charlie, trying to gain control, explained, "If you're going to dish it out, Papa, you have to be able to take it!"

"Yes, ma'am!" Papa replied **compliantly**.

"Speaking of dishing things out." Sophi looked from the pot to Mima. "How about we dish out some dump cake?"

"Good thing there wasn't much of a fire left." Papa used a small towel to grab the lid lifter out of the embers.

"Papa, would you use some of that firewood you gathered to rekindle the fire?" Mima suggested. "The girls and I need to gather a few things so we can have our cake."

"But what if he peeks," questioned Charlie.

"Oh, I think Papa has learned his lesson," replied Mima confidently. "Haven't you Papa?"

"I have learned my lesson. No peeking at magic cake!" He winked playfully, as he picked up a log.

Soon the girls were back with bowls, spoons, and whipped cream.

Papa had moved to his chair by the fire and was patiently waiting for his dessert when Mima began scooping out the syrupy goodness.

"Here you go, Maddie. You're first."

"Lucky duck." Charlie eyed Maddie's bowl.

Maddie smirked at the other two as she picked up the can and began swirling a mound of whipped cream all over the top of her warm cake.

"Don't hog it all!" Sophi shrieked.

"There's plenty for everyone," Mima assured softly.

"Besides..." Maddie handed the can to Charlie. "It melts as fast as I put it on! See...?" She tilted her bowl for all to see.

"Looks pretty darn tasty from over here!" Papa admired Maddie's handiwork. "Don't forget to bring me some!"

"Here, Papa!" Charlie handed him her steaming bowl. "You can have this one! I made it special for you! With lots of whipped cream." She smiled knowingly at Papa as she handed him the bowl.

"Aww! Thank you, Charlie!"

"That was kind of you, Charlie." Mima handed her another bowl.

Charlie grinned proudly as she took the whipped cream from Sophi and began arranging the delicious white yumminess on her new piece of cake.

"Mmm! This is SO GOOD!" Maddie inhaled deeply as a peach slipped off her spoon and back into her bowl.

"Yeah! This is the best dessert ever!" Sophi lifted her face, coming up for air long enough for everyone to see the whipped cream on the end of her nose.

They all burst out laughing.

"What's so funny?" demanded Sophi.

"Looks like you've gone headfirst to the bottom of your bowl," Papa chuckled.

Mima picked up a napkin and gently wiped it off Sophi's nose.

"I can't help it, Mima." Sophi licked the bottom of the bowl one last time. "It's delicious!"

"That's enough." Mima collected her bowl. "I'm glad you liked it!"

"You girls did a great job!" Papa slurped the last of the remnants from his spoon.

"It was magically delicious!" Maddie stated matter-of-factly. "The mini cakes that formed and the gooey syrup underneath… so magical!"

"And don't forget the melty whipped cream!" Charlie added as she finished scooping up her last bite.

"I think it should be called magic dump cake," declared Sophi.

"Then that's what we'll call it." Mima's tone was **decisive**. "Now, it's time for you ladies to get ready for bed. We had a big day today and we're doing the Ascent tomorrow."

"Great…" Charlie mumbled under her breath, clearly dreading the upcoming event.

"Yippee!" shouted Maddie. "I can't wait!"

A big yawn escaped Sophi. She didn't seem sure how she felt about the next adventure, but her tummy was full and she was getting sleepier by the minute.

"If you hurry, we'll tell a short Konfety Kingdom story to ensure sweet dreams!"

Never wanting to miss out on a chance for story time, the girls all hurried to get ready for bed, crawling into their sleeping bags just as Mima arrived to tuck them in.

Mima began the story with Rosie the unicorn meeting Jack and Jill at their usual spot on Friday afternoon. They always met and played on Saturdays, but Jack and Jill told Rosie all about how they were going on a special adventure with their Mima and Papa this Saturday, so they would see her next week and tell her all about their fun adventure!

Rosie was sad that they would be having a good time elsewhere, but she understood how special these trips were to Jack and Jill.

"It's important to spend time with your Mima and Papa," said Rosie. "Take advantage of your time together! I will see you next weekend!"

"Rosie is so thoughtful," Sophi sighed dreamily.

Mima finished her short story, gently tucked the girls in, and blew them all a goodnight kiss as she exited the tent.

"You still awake, Maddie?" Charlie whispered.

"Mmmhmm," Maddie responded softly.

"What do you think tomorrow will be like?"

"Mima always takes us on fun adventures," she said.

"But tomorrow sounds like the craziest adventure yet. I can't wait."

"Hmmm…." Charlie was reluctant. "I don't know if I want to go."

"You have to come, Charlie!" Maddie encouraged quietly. "It won't be the same without you!"

These words were like a warm hug to Charlie as she snuggled into the bottom of her sleeping bag. She still wasn't sure she wanted to go but she would talk to Papa about it in the morning.

Outside the Box

The sun was peeking through the fibers of the tent when Charlie woke up. Maddie was still sound asleep, but Sophi played with her stuffed animals, talking quietly to them as she pranced them here and there in her make-believe world.

Outside, they could hear Mima and Papa getting ready for breakfast.

"Mmmmmm! Bacon!" Sophi abandoned her stuffed **menagerie** and quickly climbed out of her sleeping bag and toward the opening.

"Race you!" Charlie opened the zipper on the tent flap and both girls shot out into the morning light.

"Is the bacon ready?" Charlie arrived at the kitchen just before Sophi.

"Bacon, BACon, BACON!" shrieked Sophi coming to a sliding halt next to Charlie.

Between laughs, Mima declared, "If I had known that was all it was going to take to get you girls out of bed, I would've started cooking thirty minutes ago!"

"Where's your cohort?" Papa attempted to control his amusement.

"What's a cohort?" Sophi reached for a piece of bacon.

"It's a friend, companion, or ally," Mima explained. "And no more bacon until breakfast is ready!"

"Can I have one too?" Charlie looked longingly at the bacon.

"Only one," Mima insisted firmly. "I know how you girls and your Papa love bacon! If you start now, you will eat it all before I have a chance to scramble the eggs."

Maddie arrived on the scene just in time to snag a piece of bacon for herself before Mima wrapped it up to keep it warm.

"Today is 'pack it all up day,'" reminded Papa.

"No way!" Maddie looked surprised. "Already?!"

"Time has passed quickly."

"At least we still have one more activity!" Mima chirped.

"Yeah," Sophi slowly agreed. "What was it called again? The Aaaassccee…"

"The As-cent," said Mima, enunciating the syllables.

"That's a hard word," declared Sophi.

"It's going to be a hard hike," Charlie grumbled.

"It'll be great!" Maddie encouraged her cousin.

"I think you'll have fun! It's like nothing you've ever done before. A new adventure!" Mima sounded like a giddy school girl.

Charlie shrugged her shoulders as she sat down at the picnic table and looked at Papa, who was busy putting away the camp chairs and cleaning up the fire pit. She desperately wanted to talk with him alone. She was sure he would understand her **trepidation**.

Soon Mima had finished scrambling the eggs and they were all at the table dishing up the warm meal.

They had all begun to eat when Sophi bolted up out of her chair.

"Oh no! We forgot the bacon!"

"It's okay, Sophi. The bacon is right here." Mima reached over to the foil wrapped package at the end of the table and opened it to reveal the salty goodness.

"Whew!" Sophi sighed as if she had nearly escaped a major **catastrophe**.

Charlie and Maddie looked at each other, then erupted with laughter at Sophi's drama.

"You'd have thought you were going to starve or something," teased Charlie.

"Yeah, it's just bacon," Maddie added as she reached for a piece.

"Just bacon!" Sophi mocked, biting off a hunk of hers and chewing loudly. "Bacon's the best!"

They all bantered back and forth as the crispy breakfast meat was passed around.

Sophi tried to snag another piece as Papa set it down.

"You've had enough, young lady," Mima gently warned. "Finish your eggs first and then you can have one more slice if you're still hungry.

As they finished up their breakfast, Papa instructed them on how they would break camp.

"I need each of you girls to roll up your sleeping bags and pack up all of your toys, books, stuffed animals, and clothes. You need to clean up your tent so we can take it down."

The girls all stared at Papa with sad eyes.

"That's going to take us forever!" Sophi pouted.

"Maybe you shouldn't have brought so much stuff," replied Maddie, ever the big sister.

"I think you can get started, and I will come and help after I get these dishes washed, packed, and ready for Papa to load into the truck."

"Okay, but hurry, Mima. I have lots to pack!" Sophi picked up her plate and headed to the sink.

The girls cleaned off their dishes, dunked them into the soapy dish water, and stumbled toward their tent.

"I'll turn on some tunes," suggested Mima.

"That would be great," Charlie agreed before she disappeared into the tent.

Soon Mima had some knee-slapping dance music jamming through the speaker on the table and the girls were giggling from inside their tent.

Mima washed the breakfast dishes while Papa rolled up his and Mima's sleeping bags and began taking down their tent, packing it all back into the truck.

Soon Mima had the make-shift kitchen ready to load and headed off to help the girls. As she approached their tent, she could hear them discussing the afternoon's event.

"It's going to be fun, Charlie," encouraged Maddie.

"How can you say that climbing a ton of stairs is going to be fun? It's going to be hard!" complained Charlie.

"What's hard is getting all my stuffed animals back in my bag!" Sophi countered, unable to see past the task at hand. "Poor Owlet is going to get squished and…"

Mima lifted the tent flap and slipped inside, bringing Maddie and Charlie's conversation to a halt.

"Yay! Mima is here! Will you help me first?" Sophi held Owlet by the wing.

Mima looked calmly at her, then glanced at her bag.

"Of course I will. Now what seems to be the problem here?"

Mima watched as Maddie and Charlie gave each other a quick glance and then continued packing their belongings, while Sophi picked up her bag of dirty clothes and dumped it all into Mima's lap.

Startled, Mima sputtered, "Whoa, Sophi! What are you doing?"

"Letting you help me!" Sophi smiled mischievously.

"Goodness." Mima shook her head in disbelief. "It's going to be quite the **feat** to get all of this to fit."

"I'm almost finished packing my bag." Maddie stuffed her last item into her bag.

"I still have my sleeping bag to roll up, and then I'm ready." Charlie zipped her bag shut.

"With Mima's help, I'll be done lickety-split!" announced Sophi.

"Well we had better get started then. How about we start with your clothes, and then we can work on the stuffed animals?" Mima reached for a pair of shorts and a shirt nearby.

Sophi started tossing her socks, shorts, jackets, and more in Mima's direction.

"Watch where you're throwing things," Maddie grumbled as a dirty sock flew right at her face.

"Yuck!" Charlie complained as Sophi launched a clothes bomb her way. "You're so lucky that didn't hit me!"

"Sophi!" Mima scolded. "You need to gather your clothes and bring them to me, not bombard us with your dirty laundry. You've made a bigger mess than when I came in to help. No one wants to dodge your dirty laundry."

"Aww… I was just having a little fun." Sophi sulked as she leaned over to pick up the items she had thrown at Maddie and Charlie and then handed them nicely to Mima.

"Thank you. That's much nicer." Mima took the pile Sophi handed to her. "Now, let's see… What might be the best way to fold these?"

Sophi collected the rest of her belongings and set them next to Mima.

"I think rolling them is going to give us the most room," decided Mima. "How about you match up your socks so we know you aren't missing any?"

"But, Mima," Maddie interrupted, "none of her socks really match."

"That's probably true! When I was a kid," Mima chuckled, **reminiscing,** "our socks always had to match whatever we were wearing."

"How boring!" Charlie held up her feet displaying her two mismatched socks.

"My, how times have changed." Mima put several socks together in pairs and packed them into the bag.

"This sleeping bag doesn't want to cooperate." Charlie was frustrated.

"Mine too." The top portion of Maddie's sleeping bag popped back out of the sack she was trying to stuff it into.

"What could you two do differently that might help you both?" Mima wondered.

Maddie and Charlie looked at each other and then shrugged their shoulders.

"What do you mean?" asked Charlie.

"I like to call it 'thinking outside of the box,'" replied Mima. "It's like a different way of doing the same thing."

"You could help us," suggested Maddie.

"Yes. That's true. But right now, I'm helping Sophi. Any other ideas?"

"Maybe we can help each other?" Charlie answered thoughtfully.

"And what would that look like?" Mima had finished packing Sophi's clothes and had moved on to the stuffed animals and other **sundries**.

Maddie thought for a moment.

"I could hold Charlie's sack for her while she stuffs the sleeping bag."

"Oh yeah!" Charlie liked this idea. "That way I don't have to do both!"

"Nice job, you two! Thinking outside of the box can help us find all kinds of different ways to make things happen."

"It's kind of like being a detective." Sophi added two stuffed animals to the pile next to Mima.

"You're exactly right, Sophi. That's a great way to explain it!"

The youngest cousin beamed quite proudly as she continued to gather her stuffed animals.

Giving their new plan a try, Maddie held the sack open while Charlie began stuffing it inside. It took a couple of tries, but when it came time to tighten the string, the bag nearly popped back out.

"Mima, can you help us, ppllleeaaasse!" Charlie pleaded as she pushed the sleeping bag back into the hole and leaned on top of it to keep it from exploding out the top.

"On my way!" Mima sprang up from the pile of Sophi's animals to help Maddie hold the sack together while Charlie secured the strings.

"Whew! That was so exhausting!" Charlie flopped down onto the tent floor. "I think I used all my energy just wrapping up that sleeping bag."

"It sure is easier to get them out than to stuff them in!" Maddie observed as she reached for hers.

"Nice work, you two!" congratulated Mima, silently taking note of Charlie's comment and then responding, "One bag down, one to go!"

Mima understood that Charlie was hesitant about this next adventure, but she also knew what Charlie was capable of. It was going to be a great opportunity for Charlie to see herself in a different light.

"At least this time, I get to do the holding." Charlie picked up the sack so Maddie could work on her sleeping bag.

"Okay, Sophi." Mima sat back down to help. "I think we have almost completed this project. What else do we have to pack?"

"Just my kindle and Owlet" Sophi handed both items to Mima.

"Awesome!" congratulated Mima. "I think we're done!"

"Whew!" sighed Sophi.

"Hold tight, Charlie," Maddie warned as she began shoving wads of the sleeping bag into the sack.

"Don't push so hard, Maddie!" Charlie gasped, her grip slipping. "You're pushing the sack right out of my hands!"

Maddie slowed down to give Charlie a chance to grab hold again.

"Okay, Sophi. Your turn. I'll hold the bag and you stuff it in."

Sophi took hold of her sleeping bag and pushed one end into the bag, but as she pulled her hands back out, the sleeping bag came out too.

"Mima!" Sophi stomped her foot in frustration after the second try ended with the same results. "I can't do it!" She whined and stomped her foot again.

"Uh oh," cautioned Maddie. "I see a temper tantrum coming on!"

Charlie nodded her head in agreement.

Mima looked at the girls sternly.

"How might you two be of help here?"

"This sounds like another test of our 'think outside of the box' skills." Charlie looked at Maddie for confirmation.

"Yeah." Maddie pretended to put on her super-sleuth hat and tapped her chin thoughtfully.

Mima couldn't help but smile.

"You girls…" She shook her head at their silly play.

"I suppose," began Charlie, "Maddie and I could hold the sack and you could help Sophi."

"I like that idea!" Sophi quickly turned her frown upside-down, a big smile spreading across her face.

"Let's give it a try." Maddie handed part of the sack to Charlie, while she held the other side.

Sophi picked up the end of the sleeping bag and shoved it to the bottom of the sack, firmly instructing it, "Stay!"

As she pulled her hands out, Mima was ready with the next portion. Taking her turn, she pushed the fabric down inside.

They continued this process until the sleeping bag was finally fully contained and the cord had been securely tied on top.

"Great job!" Mima gave each of them a high-five. "You did it!"

"How are you ladies doing?" Papa poked his head into the tent flap.

"Look, Papa!" Sophi proudly held her hand out and spun in a circle.

"Wow! Look at you girls go!" Papa smiled. Their faces brightened at his praise.

"What's next, Papa?" asked Charlie.

"How about each of you grab your bundles and haul them over to the truck so I can load them?"

"You might have to make a couple of trips." Mima took a minute to look at the piles in the tent.

Maddie and Charlie grabbed their duffle bags and started for the tent door.

"Wait for me." Sophi grabbed her backpack and followed them.

As soon as Papa placed the rest of the luggage and sleeping bags outside the tent, Mima grabbed her broom and began sweeping out all the dirt, leaves, and grass that had made its way inside the tent.

"Look what I found!" Mima poked her head out of the tent and held up a book of Maddie's, a sock belonging to Charlie, and Sophi's pajama top and slipper.

"Oh my!" Maddie's eyes were wide with surprise. "Where did you find that?"

"All of these items were in the spare room."

"No way." Charlie reached for her sock. "I'm sure I looked in there!"

"I think you must have hid them, Mima." A sly grin spread across Sophi's face.

"You think so, do you?" Mima gave Sophi a playful wink. "I think you three had best put them in those last bags of yours so they make it home with you."

The girls managed to get all of the lost and found items into their bags and lugged them off to the truck. When they came back, it was time to help Papa take down the tent.

Papa began showing the girls how to do it effectively.

"We just do everything in reverse."

The girls helped him remove the support poles and the stakes.

"Grrr… This is so hard," Sophi squeaked between clenched teeth as she tried to pull up one of the stakes.

"I agree!" Charlie gave her stake one more hard pull, causing it to pop out and fly into the air, and her to fall down to the ground, landing on her bottom with a thud.

"Ouch!" exclaimed Maddie as if she were the one that had fallen. "Are you okay?" She went over to help her cousin up off the ground.

Papa had the rest of the stakes pulled out by the time the chaos had settled down. He taught them how to fold the tent and put it back into the bag along with the poles.

"Always make sure you keep it all together. That way, you always know you have all of the pieces."

"You sound like Daddy," Maddie giggled.

"Yeah." Sophi shook her head in agreement.

"Well," snickered Mima. "We might have said that a few times to him when he was a kid, especially about picking up his toys."

Maddie and Sophi both giggled at the thought of their daddy as a kid, being told to pick up his toys.

Charlie, however, noticed that Papa was headed to the truck with the tent and scurried after him, leaving her cousins and Mima to their banter.

The Struggle is Real

"Hey, Papa! Wait for me," Charlie broke into a jog to catch up with him.

Hearing her call him, Papa stopped and waited.

"What's up?" He waited a moment for her to catch her breath.

"Can we talk?" she asked shyly.

"Of course! What seems to be on your mind?"

"It's about the stairs," Charlie admitted as she twisted her hair nervously.

Papa hefted the tent into the back of his truck and turned to give Charlie his full attention.

"What about the stairs?"

"It sounds like there are a lot of stairs…" Charlie began again.

"Ah-hmmm."

"And they are steep, right?"

"There are a lot of stairs and it's pretty steep, but what seems to be the problem?" he coaxed.

"I don't… I don't… Ummm… I don't think I can make it," she stuttered.

"It will probably be difficult, but Mima wouldn't have chosen this hike if she didn't think you could do it," Papa encouraged.

"But… You don't have to do it… Why do I?" she rebutted.

"Charlie, you know Papa has two bad knees that won't allow me to climb. You have two strong legs! You can do it!" he attempted to reassure her.

"But what if I can't?" Charlie nearly burst into tears.

"Just give it a try." Papa put his arm around her shoulders and gave her an encouraging squeeze. Then he bent over and looked Charlie straight in the eyes. "I'm sure that Mima will take it slow and you ladies can always come down if it gets too hard." Then standing back up, he repeated, "Mima wouldn't ask you to do something she didn't believe you could do."

Charlie sighed and walked away, her shoulders slumped.

"What am I going to do now?" she softly whispered to herself. "I thought for sure Papa would understand and not make me go." She hung her head in defeat.

"There you are." Maddie stopped abruptly as Charlie nearly bumped into her. "I wondered where you'd gone."

Charlie sighed.

"I went to talk with Papa. I just don't see how I can climb more than twenty, or thirty stairs, and definitely not hundreds!" A tear escaped and ran down her cheek. "You and Sophi both play soccer, so it's easier for you." Charlie wiped the wetness from her face. "And what if I break a shoelace, and you don't realize I'm not with you, and I get left behind, and then I lose my way?"

Before Maddie could interject a calming word, Charlie continued her frenzy of questions.

"What if my legs won't let me climb one more stair? Will Mima still love me? Will she be disappointed?"

Charlie plopped heavily onto a large rock and put her head in her hands. Maddie put a loving arm around her cousin.

"Mima loves adventures, and this one will be tough." Maddie attempted to comfort her cousin. "But Mima believes in all of us, and she would never leave one of us behind."

"I don't know, Maddie." Charlie shook her head in disbelief. "These butterflies in my tummy think differently."

Busted

Charlie was sulking back into camp just as Papa announced, "I believe we're packed and ready to go!"

Mima suggested they all walk around the campsite one more time to make sure there wasn't any trash or items left behind.

"You mean like books, socks, and pajamas?" Papa teased.

"Papa!" Sophi shot back with a glare.

"Alright, ladies and gentleman," began Mima. "Let's each take a section and double check. Even if it is a piece of trash that's not ours, we want to leave the campsite better than we found it."

They did find a few small pieces of paper on the ground and a paper towel that had been caught in a bush and threw them away.

"I think we got it all!" Maddie dropped her trash into the garbage.

Papa tied up the bag and put it into the back of the truck.

"Pack it in… pack it out," he chanted as they all climbed into the truck.

"What a great trip!" Sophi stared out Charlie's window as she watched the campsite disappear behind them.

"And the best is yet to come!" Maddie exclaimed excitedly. "How far is it to the Ascent?"

"Only about thirty minutes." Mima checked her watch to see what time they would arrive.

"Just enough time to read." Maddie opened her book and found where she had left off.

"Or eat!" suggested Sophi.

Charlie stared intently out her window, looking worried.

"Funny you should mention food. I have sandwiches for us to eat so that we're all fueled for our hike."

"Yummy," said Sophi, reaching for a PB & J.

"Yours is on a tortilla, Maddie, with very little peanut butter." Mima winked in Maddie's direction.

"Thanks, Mima." Maddie reached for her wrap.

"Hey, Charlie! Would you like a sandwich?"

Charlie pulled her focus away from the window and reached for her lunch.

"You looked like you were deep in thought." Mima smiled at Charlie. "What were you thinking about?"

"The hike," Charlie muttered as she took a big bite out of her sandwich.

"You're going to do great!" Mima expressed her belief in Charlie's abilities.

"Hmm…" Charlie was still unsure.

"These are great sandwiches, Mima." Papa tried to change the topic of the conversation. "I'm so glad you packed them for us!"

"I agggrrree," Sophi slurred, her mouth full of sticky peanut butter and jelly.

It wasn't long before Papa turned off the highway and down the road to the trailhead.

The parking lot was nearly full of cars, but Papa found a space toward the back where he could watch for the ladies as they hiked back down.

Mima grabbed her backpack and encouraged the girls to follow her.

"Let's take a picture at the trailhead before we start."

As they approached the Ascent, the trail of old railroad ties transformed into stairs came into full view.

Charlie looked up and gulped.

"This is going to be impossible," she mumbled under her breath.

Reaching the trailhead, Mima gathered the girls around her for a picture before heading toward the top.

"Say 'cheeseburgers,'" Papa encouraged smiles and giggles.

But Charlie was not in the mood to smile.

"Mima," she called.

Pausing on the first stair, Mima turned to look at Charlie.

"Yes, Charlie?"

"Papa said I didn't have to do the hike if I didn't want to." Charlie stared at her feet.

Mima's eyes turned to find Papa's, questioning why he would do that.

Before Mima could say anything, Papa jumped in, "Oh, now wait a minute, Charlie. That's not what I said."

Mima looked from Papa to Charlie, and back to Papa again.

"I told you that you needed to try and that if you couldn't make it, Mima would bring you back down."

Charlie hung her head. She was busted and she knew it.

Doing Hard Things

Mima lifted Charlie's chin.

"You know Mima loves you very much, right?"

The middle cousin looked at Mima and nodded her head.

"And I would never ask you to do something that I didn't believe you could do."

"I guess not." Charlie shrugged her shoulders.

"This is going to be hard, but you can do hard things! All three of you can!" Mima looked at all three girls. "I believe in you girls. And…" Mima paused to

look directly into Charlie's eyes, "if you can't make it...
it's okay. But I want you to try."

Recognizing her continued reluctance, Mima suggested, "How about we try doing just one hundred
steps?" Mima paused for the idea to sink in. "When
we reach one hundred, we'll stop and you can get a
drink. If you can't make it, we'll come back down.
Would you be willing to try that and see how it
goes?"

"I guess..." Charlie answered hesitantly.

Mima gave her an encouraging hug and held her
hand as they waved goodbye to Papa and started up the
trail slowly counting, "One, two, three..."

Encouraged along the way with, "Good job!" and
"You're nearly there," they soon were counting, "ninety-
eight, ninety-nine, ONE HUNDRED!"

"Look at you go!" Mima pulled water bottles out of
her backpack for each of them.

"That was so hard!" Charlie grumbled.

"Yes, it was, but I bet you girls have another one
hundred steps in you."

"I do!" Sophi confirmed.

"That was fun." Maddie looked up. "I'm ready to
do more!"

Charlie wasn't thrilled, but she agreed to do one
hundred more.

"And look," offered Mima enthusiastically as she pointed to the number 100 painted on the railroad tie. "Looks like we won't even have to count the logs. They have already been marked for us!"

"Yay!" Maddie cheered.

"This is a steep incline, so we'll keep going slow and steady on this next set of steps," Mima instructed.

They set off again and before they knew it, they had climbed two hundred steps.

After another rest and drink of water, Mima looked at Charlie. "I believe you can go another one hundred steps. What do you think?"

"This is not easy!" Charlie whined.

"No, it's probably not the easiest thing we've ever done, " Mima agreed. "But I believe we can all make it another set of steps." Then she turned to Sophi. "What do you think, Sophi?"

"It was pretty hard, but I think we can do another set."

"Let's do it!" Maddie was excited and clearly enjoying the adventure.

"You don't have to be in such a hurry," Charlie scowled.

"It's okay that Maddie is excited, and it's okay that you're not." Mima looked from one granddaughter to the other. "You each get to choose to enjoy this or to be miserable."

"But it's really hard, Mima!" Charlie argued.

"I understand, but let's climb another one hundred steps and see how we do."

Dragging her feet, Charlie continued to climb. Pretty soon, she noticed a small ground squirrel.

"Look, Mima." She pointed at the small animal as he scampered away. "He looks so soft and cuddly!"

"He's a cutie!"

Maddie reached step three hundred first and declared, "Here it is!"

"Whew! Made it," Sophi added, only a few steps behind Maddie.

"Nicely done," Mima encouraged from several steps below. "Charlie and I are on our way!"

"Good job, Charlie!" Maddie cheered as Mima and Charlie reached them.

They took a small break and drank some more water. When everyone had rested, Mima laid out the challenge of another set.

"Let's go for four hundred. What do you say?"

"Mima, that is so many steps!" Charlie moaned and took another drink of water.

"Yes, but I think we should try," cheered Mima. "This is just like life. It's not easy, but we're all stronger than we think we are."

Again they climbed, making it to step four hundred where they again had a short break and a drink of water.

"Guess what I have if we make it to step five hundred?" Mima swung her backpack from side to side.

"What's our big surprise?" Sophi enthusiastically shouted.

"Yeah, tell us Mima," insisted Maddie.

Charlie stared at Mima, looking unsure.

"When we make it to five hundred, Mima has treats!"

"Treats." Charlie sighed loudly. "What kind of treats?"

"Treats, treats, treats!" Sophi chanted.

"I have all kinds of treats," began Mima. "I have suckers, jerky, animal crackers, fruit snacks, candies, pretzels, and more."

"Which one do we get first?" asked Charlie.

"You choose," said Mima. "There's enough for everyone to have at least one of each. And, I have more water bottles."

"Can I run up to number five hundred and wait for you there?" Maddie asked as she moved the dirt around with the toe of her shoe.

"Absolutely," encouraged Mima. "Just make sure you stop there to wait for the rest of us."

"Can I go with her?" Sophi asked as Maddie took off.

"Sure!" answered Mima, but Sophi was already running after her big sister.

"Come on, Charlie," Mima encouraged, reaching for her hand. "Let's do this together."

Charlie reached for Mima's hand and let Mima pull her up off the log.

"They are so much better at this!" Charlie pouted.

"Maddie and Charlie both play soccer and you haven't had the opportunity to play sports," Mima acknowledged. "Have you been walking like we talked about?"

"Some," said Charlie. "But not a bunch of stairs!"

Mima smiled, understanding her frustration.

After several steps, Charlie and Mima looked up to see where Maddie and Sophi were.

"Look! Maddie is already there," Charlie growled. "And Sophi's not far behind."

"And we'll be there shortly," encouraged Mima.

Mima was right. It wasn't long before they were all sitting together on the five hundredth step and Mima pulled out a gallon sized bag filled with treats.

"What would you like from my goodie bag?"

"Oh!" Sophi hungrily eyed the treats. "I want it all!"

"No, Sophi," Charlie snapped. "You only get to have one."

"But Mima said there were enough for us to have one of each." Sophi sniffled as she looked up at Mima for confirmation.

"I did say that," Mima admitted. "However, I didn't say you could have them all at once."

"Darn!" Sophi picked out a sucker. "I want this pink one."

Maddie and Charlie both chose their snacks, and all three cousins sat down on the log to eat their yummy rewards.

Gathering up the girls' wrappers, Mima put them in her pack and then zipped it shut.

"What do you think of this plan?" The girls all stared intently at Mima. "We'll stop every one hundred steps and get a drink. Then, at every five hundred steps, we have a treat. Sound good?"

"Let's do it!" Maddie was thrilled.

"I like snacks!" Sophi noisily licked her sucker. "Can we have them at every stop?"

"Nope! The snacks have to be earned." Mima smiled slyly.

"Of course you want to," Charlie growled under her breath. "I can't believe you call this fun! It's so hard!"

"Lots of things are hard, Charlie," Mima coached lovingly. "It's how you deal with the hard that allows you to still have fun or to be miserable. I know that you can do hard things! But only you can decide *how* you will do them."

Everyone agreed to continue on, and Maddie led them up the steep incline, reaching the next stopping point well before the others.

Mima kept an eye on Maddie's climb as she encouraged Sophi and Charlie along the way.

It was actually a big help that Maddie would get to the next marker and sit, helping the gang to know where the next stop would be.

About half-way up, some folks stopped to talk to the girls.

"You kids sure are doing a great job!" a lady encouraged.

It wasn't until the man turned to talk to the girls that they realized he had a parrot on his shoulder.

"Oh, look!" Sophi squealed with delight as she pointed at the bird perched proudly on his owner's shoulder.

"What's his name?" Maddie inquired.

"Can we pet him?" added Charlie.

"Whoa, slow down girls," encouraged Mima.

The man chuckled at the girls' enthusiasm.

"His name is George, and he just loves walking and hiking with me!"

Lifting George gently off his shoulder, he looked the parrot in the eyes.

"These lovely ladies would like to pet you, George. Would that be okay?"

"Lovely ladies… lovely ladies…" George chirped as he bobbed his head up and down to the entertainment of all around.

The man held George down to where the girls could all reach his back and one at a time, they stroked him gently.

"Pretty George," Charlie cooed at him softly.

"Pretty George," the bird loudly squawked.

"Does he ever fly away?" Sophi was amazed that he was sitting so patiently.

"No, not out here. George knows he's safe with me, so he just stays here on my shoulder."

"That's so cool!" Charlie was delighted.

"Thanks for letting us pet him." Mima nodded at the nice man.

"Have a good hike." The man placed George back on his shoulder and continued on his way.

"Thank you!" chorused the girls after him.

"I love you, George!" called Sophi. Then giggling, she sprung up another step.

Chattering about the bird made the next hundred steps go by quickly.

"How fun was that?" Mima questioned as they neared the next stop.

"That was crazy, seeing George riding on that man's shoulder!" Maddie marched quickly.

"I can't believe he just stays there." Charlie was overcome with fascination and wonder.

"I can't wait to tell Daddy!" Sophi excitedly mounted several stairs.

"Our dad's aren't going to believe this!" Charlie shook her head from side to side, still in awe.

They continued to chatter as they drank some water before starting toward the **summit**.

During the next several sets of stairs, they found additional wildlife.

"Look at all these ants." Sophi stopped momentarily to investigate a pile of red ants.

"Wow!" Charlie pointed to one particular ant that caught her attention. "That one is carrying a huge crumb of something, like maybe a granola bar?"

"Yeah," agreed Sophi.

"Come on, girls. Let's keep it moving. Maddie is already up at the next rest area."

"Maddie is always there before we are," groaned Sophi.

Charlie shot one more glance at the ants before stepping up onto the next log.

"Any idea what number the step is that Maddie is sitting on?" Mima wondered out loud.

The girls both shook their heads back and forth, as if saying, "No," would take too much effort.

Sighs and grumbles followed Mima as she stayed just a step or two ahead.

When they finally reached Maddie, she was stretched out with her shoes perched on top of the step number.

"What step are we on, Maddie?" Mima obviously already knew the answer.

"Hmm…" Maddie scooted her feet out of the way, revealing the total steps climbed. "Two thousand one hundred."

"Holy cow!" Charlie slumped down onto the log next to Maddie. "It's no wonder I'm exhausted."

"I definitely need a snack." Sophi plopped down next to Maddie.

"But you just had one." Mima chuckled at Sophi's determination to snag an extra snack.

"Are we getting close to the top?" Maddie took a large gulp from her water bottle.

"Well," hesitated Mima. "If you look up, it appears that the summit is just above us, but don't let that fool you."

"What do you mean 'fool us'?" Charlie looked toward the landing.

"It's what is known as a false summit."

"What's a false summit?" Maddie squinted up to follow Mima's gaze.

"That means that it looks like you'll reach the top, but when you get there, you find out you're not quite there." Mima placed her bottle back in the side pocket of her pack.

"Oh no!" Charlie fussed wearily.

"That's just mean!" Sophi stomped her foot. "You mean ol' mountain!"

"We actually have maybe six more stops before we reach the top," Mima estimated.

"Six more!" Charlie whined. "My legs are tired. Can't we go down now?"

"You don't really want to go down now, do you?" Mima asked. "You're so close to the top!"

"We don't want to quit now," championed Maddie.

"Come on, let's climb the next set of stairs and get over the top of that ledge." Mima looked at the girls with admiration. "I'm positive you have enough left in you to make it! I know it's hard, but you are stronger than you think you are!"

Charlie grumbled as she climbed the next few stairs.

"Hey, there's a chipmunk!" Sophi gave them another excuse to stop and watch a tiny creature scuttle around.

Charlie knelt down and held out her hand.

"Here little chipmunk!" The fuzzy ball of fur scurried up a step and over to the other side. "Ahh…" Charlie sighed as she climbed another step.

"He was so cute. I was hoping we could catch him. Then I could take him home." Sophi clapped her hands together, pretending to capture the tiny creature.

"We don't want to take the animal out of its habitat. His family would miss him and you don't want them to be sad." Mima attempted to steer their focus away from the stairs and onto the chipmunk.

Charlie dragged her feet toward the next step.

"Some of these stairs are so tall and hard to climb."

Sophi slipped her hand into Charlie's.

"Come on, Charlie, I'll help you!"

Mima beamed with pride as she watched Sophi help Charlie up the next few stairs. "That's so sweet of you, Sophi. I know you're tired, but working together will help us all make it to the top. Nice job!"

They continued to make their way slowly up the trail, one step at a time, stopping for a rest and a drink of water at each marked step.

"Look!" Mima pointed up the mountain twenty steps to where Maddie had just sat down. "There's our next rest stop!"

There was some muttering behind her as she turned to see Charlie and Sophi side by side trudging up the hill, talking quietly to each other.

Reaching Maddie, Mima pulled off her backpack and opened it up.

"Step number two thousand five hundred. You know what that means!"

"SNACKS!" Sophi raced up the last step and grabbed a granola bar from the display Mima had set out.

Maddie chose fruit snacks and Charlie decided on some jerky.

They were all chatting when Mima commented, "It sure is beautiful up here!"

Charlie stood up to get a better view. Having been so focused on the difficulty of the hike, she suddenly realized she hadn't paid any attention to how far up they had climbed. As she looked out at the beauty before her, Charlie gasped and turned around so quickly, she nearly knocked Mima over in her excitement.

"Mima!" she cried, her eyes filled with amazement and accomplishment as she looked down. "I didn't know I could make it this far!"

Mima took Charlie's face tenderly between her hands, leaned down, and looked directly into her big, beautiful brown eyes, dancing with excitement.

"Yes! Look at what you have done!" Then she gave her face a gentle squeeze. "I want you to always remember, YOU are stronger than you think you are and YOU can do hard things!"

Charlie nearly jumped up and down with renewed energy and anticipation that was contagious, allowing the last leg of the hike to go much more quickly.

At the last water break, they could see the top, only forty-four steps away.

"Let's do this, shall we?" Mima grinned widely at all three girls.

Exhausted and ready to finish, they began the last of the climb to the summit.

With only twenty steps left to climb and several people at the top cheering them on, the girls all grabbed hands and ran to the summit.

"You did it!" shouted one hiker.

Other hikers congratulated them and asked how old they were.

"I'm five-and-a-half," announced Sophi proudly.

"We're eight and nearly nine." Maddie gave Charlie a minute to catch her breath.

"We've never seen kids your age hike this before." Another hiker celebrated their arrival at the top.

Mima wrapped her arms around all three girls.

"How about a picture here at the top of the Ascent and then you can have a snack before we head back down the hill?"

"Are we going back down the stairs?" Sophi eagerly reached for another sucker.

"Not today." Mima chuckled. "Those steps are more difficult to go down than they are to come up. It would be easy, especially as tired as we are, to get dizzy, trip, and fall. We'll take the back way down."

"Whew!" Charlie exclaimed wearily. "I don't think I would want to climb down all those steps!"

Maddie breathed a sigh of relief, which prompted Mima to ask her a question.

"So, Maddie," began Mima, "you sure went up those steps lickety-split. Why did you want to run them?" Mima thought she was showing off her soccer running skills.

"I was thinking outside of the box," she responded slyly.

"What do you mean by that?" Mima was surprised at her response.

Maddie pretended to adjust her super-sleuth hat.

"I figured if I could get up the steps first, I would have longer to rest while I waited for you to reach me!"

Mima gave Maddie a proud wink and, with a hearty chuckle, congratulated her on a job well done.

Lost in Celebration

"You've all done a magnificent job today!" Mima gushed. "I think it's time to head back down the mountain and see if Papa and your dads are waiting for us."

"Yippee!" Sophi threw her fist up into the air. "I can't wait to see Daddy and tell him all about the bats that live in the cave and the story of the princess."

"And I want to tell him about our parrot friend, George, we met on the trail today, and how I caught Papa trying to sneak some of the dump cake," Maddie reminisced.

"Ooh, and how the North Star is part of the Little Dipper, and Papa pretending to be a bear on our hike!" Charlie paused and wrinkled her brow. "I'm glad it was girls only! We wouldn't have done any of these fun things if my two baby brothers had come."

"It's true. They are still too little for such big adventures, but eventually," Mima continued, "they will get to join in on our Cousin Camps and experience Papa and his crazy antics too."

Charlie stared momentarily at Mima with her big brown eyes and then sighed deeply, "I guess I did miss them just a little bit."

Mima hugged Charlie's shoulder and turned her attention back to the moment.

"Come on, ladies! Let's go!"

And down the trail they went.

They had been hiking along for only a few minutes when they came across a log lying across the trail.

Mima paused for a moment and pondered the sight before her.

"That's strange." She could hear other voices nearby and assumed they were on the trail. "Hmmm… I don't see any other trail, so let's climb over this log and continue on."

Each of the girls climbed over, and together they continued walking. They had hiked several minutes more and hadn't seen anyone. The **terrain** was pretty rough and Mima was beginning to worry that she had led the girls **astray**.

A few minutes later, Charlie stopped and looked around.

"I think we're lost!"

Maddie, wondering where Mima was leading them, agreed, "Yeah! We're definitely lost!"

"You're not really lost, are you, Mima?" Sophi sounded concerned.

"No, we're not lost," Mima confirmed. "What are some things we could do if perhaps we did go the wrong way?

"I don't want to be lost," declared Sophi.

"We're not lost," Mima calmly reminded. "Do you know how I know?"

The girls all looked at Mima and shook their heads.

"I have on my super-sleuth hat."

The girls all rolled their eyes.

"Come on, Mima," whined Sophi.

Recognizing that the girls were getting tired, Mima suggested, "Let's sit for a minute and have a snack."

"Snacks!" Sophi found some hidden energy.

The girls each picked out one more snack from Mima's backpack and sat down on a rock to listen.

"You ready?" asked Mima.

"Um hmm..." replied Sophi, her mouth full of licorice.

"First of all, I know where we've been. So as a last resort, we could turn around and go back up the trail to the log, cross over the log, and go back to where we started. There were several people still coming up the mountain, others that were enjoying the view at the top, and I saw a park ranger talking with other hikers. He would know where we went wrong and help us find the right trail."

"But I don't want to go all the way back," grumbled Charlie.

"We don't have to. I said that would be the last resort, meaning the last thing we would do."

"Whew!" Charlie sighed.

"So, how do you know we aren't lost?" Maddie looked at Mima.

"Listen."

The girls stopped eating their snacks for a moment and listened intently.

Charlie's eyes brightened.

"I hear voices."

"Me too!" Maddie popped the last of her granola bar into her mouth.

"Correct. Those voices are getting louder and louder, which means they are getting closer and closer.

Let's keep going, just a little bit further."

Mima gathered their wrappers, put them into her backpack, and led them down the path.

They had only gone about one hundred steps when their trail dead ended into another trail.

Taking this moment to help the girls use their super-sleuth skills, she asked, "Which way do you think we should go?"

"That way!" Sophi pointed to the right.

"You're correct, but why would you go that way?" Mima figured she had just made a lucky guess.

Sophi shrugged her shoulders, confirming Mima's suspicion.

"What do you two think?" Mima looked at Maddie and Charlie. "Why should we go to the right?"

"If we go to the right," began Charlie, "it looks like we're going downhill."

"And, going downhill should lead us to the bottom of the mountain." Maddie looked at Mima for confirmation.

"That's true usually, but most of the time trails go up and down with the terrain, so you can't always assume down is going to continue down to the trailhead. However… do you hear what I hear?"

"People!" Sophi shouted, relief spreading across her face.

Around the corner and toward them came several hikers laughing and joking, and moving rather quickly.

"Let's step to the side and let them pass us since we're not quite as fast." Mima waved as the hikers maneuvered past them.

Once the hikers passed them, Mima and the girls headed down the trail, passing some and being passed by others. Knowing they were on the right trail made everyone happier.

Pretty soon, the dirt trail turned into a paved path leading through the last few twists and turns.

As they were rounding a corner, Mima recognized a voice hollering up at them: "What are you doing way up there?"

"Did you hear that?" Mima halted.

"That sounded like Daddy!" cried Sophi. "But where is he?"

The girls searched the grounds below.

"Come on. We're almost there!" Mima continued downhill.

As they rounded another corner, two familiar faces popped into view.

"Daddy!" shouted all three girls as they ran toward their fathers.

"Oh, Daddy!" Sophi ran and threw her arms around him. "You won't believe all of the adventures we've had! We went to a cave and bats live there, but there was this princess and…"

Charlie reached her dad and began her tale of their travels.

"We were out hiking and Papa pretended to be a bear and…"

Not to be left out, Maddie chimed in with her version of their adventures.

"And there was this parrot on the trail, and his name was George!"

"Whoa…" Charlie's dad motioned for them to slow down. "You're all talking at once!"

"One at a time," suggested Maddie and Sophi's dad.

"Youngest goes first," Sophi announced playfully.

They chatted the last little bit down the trail, each taking a turn until they reached Papa.

"Yay! You all made it!" Papa celebrated their arrival. "And because you all made it, I have a surprise for you!"

"What is it? What is it?" Charlie squealed.

Papa pulled a paper bag out from behind his back and held it up above their reach.

"Come on, Papa!" Maddie groaned. "Stop teasing!"

Papa grinned widely as he pulled three shirts out of his bag, and the girls all ran over to him.

"What does it say?" Sophi furrowed her brow.

"The best views come from the hardest climbs," read Papa.

"Boy, you can say that again!" Charlie took a deep breath.

"Do you want to share your discovery with Papa and the others?" Mima gently nudged Charlie.

Charlie dug her toe into the dirt.

"It was really, really hard, Papa! I didn't think I could keep going. I wanted to give up so many times." She turned toward Mima who smiled back encouragingly and nodded for her to continue. "Thank goodness, we stopped for water and snacks! Near the top, I was eating my snack when I looked down and saw how far we had hiked. I couldn't believe I had made it so far, Papa! It was so beautiful and amazing! It felt so good, and I was able to make it all the way to the top!

"I'm so proud of you, Charlie!" congratulated Papa. "You stuck with it, and that's important."

"Yes!" Mima moved over to stand next to Papa. "Life is hard, but it's how we attack it that makes the difference. All three of you chose to do something really hard today. You pushed through, encouraged each other, and made it to the top and back down together."

"Nicely done, everyone!" congratulated Maddie and Sophi's dad.

"I'm impressed with all you girls." Charlie's dad hugged her proudly. "I hate to break up this party, but I'll bet these ladies are hungry. You can only eat so many snacks."

"Me! Me! I am!" Sophi bounded toward her uncle.

"How about we all go get some pizza and celebrate your success!" suggested Papa.

"Pizza!" Charlie was thrilled.

"That sounds amazing!" Maddie patted her belly hungrily.

Sitting around the table at the pizzeria, cheese dripping off her chin, Maddie exclaimed, "This has been so much fun! I can't wait to see what our next adventure is!"

"Um hmm," agreed Charlie, smacking her lips at the cheesy goodness.

"I hope it includes pizza!" laughed Sophi.

"And no stairs!" Charlie winked at Mima as she popped the last bite of her pizza into her mouth.

Glossary

admonition - gentle or friendly warning

affirmed / affirmatively - To state positively

antics - horseplay/foolish, outrageous, or amusing behavior

array – an impressive display (in this case, color)

astray – away from the correct path

bandwagon - an activity that is currently popular and attracting support

bantered - to speak in a teasing manner

beeline - a direct route traveled quickly

befalling - something bad happening to someone

cadence - a rhythmic sequence or flow of sounds in language

canvassed - looked around

catastrophe - a momentous tragic event

chagrin - disappointment

chastened - disciplined

chortled - to laugh or chuckle

clamored – in a loud manner

clan - family

cohort - a group of people with shared characteristics

compliantly - obediently

conceded - gave in

concurred - agreed

conjured - brought forth or used

contagious - tending to spread from person to person

culprit - person responsible

dastardly - unpleasant task

decisive - firm

dejectedly - in a way that shows unhappiness or disappointment

delectable - delightful or enjoyable

elegance - cultivated beauty

elevation - the height above the level of the sea

embedded - planted

emphasis - a force of expression that gives importance to something

emphatically - powerful or loud speech

enamored - captivated

entourage - group of people

exasperated – very irritated and frustrated

farce - a ridiculous or absurd situation that is intended to make people laugh

feat - an achievement that requires great courage, skill, or strength

feigned - pretend to be

gallant - brave

hangry - hungry and angry

hypothesis - assumption

intuitively - gut feeling

Irish twins – two children born in approximately twelve months of each other

levitated - to rise or float into the air

Konfety - the Russian pronunciation for candy

Konfety Kingdom - a make-believe land made of sugary treats and filled with magical creatures

mayhem - a state of rowdy disorder

menagerie - a variety or mixture

merriment - light hearted gaiety or fun-making

morsels - a small piece of food

nonchalantly - in a casual, calm, and relaxed manner

ornery - difficult to deal with or control

paraphernalia - personal belongings

phenomena - a rare or significant fact or event

quandary - a state of doubt

reluctantly - with hesitation

regulate - control

reminiscing - to enjoy thinking about past events

remorse - deep regret or guilt for wrongdoing

replenishes - to make full again

resolutely - in a determined or firm manner

reverberates - a noise repeated several times as in an echo

sauntered - to walk at a slow pace, to stroll

scheming - involved in making secret plans

scrounged - seek out

scrutinizing - to examine or inspect closely and thoroughly

sedimentary - mineral or organic matter deposited by water, air, or ice to create a formation

shenanigans - silly or high-spirited behavior, mischief

shrapnel – small pieces of metal that fly through the air when a bomb explodes

simultaneously – at the same time

sleuthing - detective work

soda - soft drink or pop

sulked - to remain silent, to mope

summit - the highest point of a hill or mountain

sundries - a variety of items not important enough to be mentioned individually

taut - stretched or pulled tight

tentatively - to hesitate, be unsure or uncertain

terrain - a stretch of land, especially in regard to its physical features

trepidation - a feeling of fear or agitation about something that may happen

thwart - to prevent someone from accomplishing something

unison - two or more people saying the same thing at the same time

wafted - to carry lightly or smoothly through the air

A Special Invitation from Mima

Ready to bring the adventure home?

We've been busy having fun over here at Cousin Camp,
creating games, puzzles, scavenger hunts, prompts, and more
to help you find adventure wherever you are.

As you wait to see what Maddie, Charlie, and Sophi
do in their next adventure,
have some fun playing one of our adventure games,
creating a Konfety Kingdom adventure,
or completing one of our Mile Marker Maps.

www.Cousin-Camp-Chronicles.com

About Mima

Lori Giesey

Mima enjoys creating and participating in high-adventure team opportunities where individuals learn that the choice to create and live your own highest adventure is a lot easier and a lot more fun and rewarding than just letting life happen to you.

Her push-myself-further adventures include participating in marathons, ultra-marathons, triathlon races, and writing. Through all of her writing and adventures, Mima seeks to inspire and empower both young and old to reach higher, go further, and become more than they ever imagined.

Lori loves traveling with her husband and best friend, Mike, and they have recently found their perfect spot in the Black Hills of South Dakota where they are creating their own special family haven.

Acknowledgments

To the Co-Author...

who whispered in my ear, "You are enough."

To My Family...

To my husband, Mike, for being my BFF, my safe place to land, for helping me to stay grounded and focused, and for coming along on yet another adventure. Adventure is always sweeter with you by my side!

To my sister, Tammy, for your willingness to read and reread and share your many years of experience working with children with this project. Your friendship and companionship have made a world of difference.

To All of My Past and Present Teachers, Mentors, and Coaches...

To those who saw and nurtured my spirit.

Amanda, thank you for seeing all of me, and helping me to dig deep, rework old stories, create new contracts, step outside my comfort zone, and reach for the stars! I couldn't have done this without you!

To My Team...

To those who added their talents to this creation...

Brylee Allred, thank you for being willing to take a leap with me to share your creative talents with the world at sixteen. You saved this series! I love and respect you for the time and effort you put into each illustration, for sharing your ideas, and for being teachable. You, my young friend, are amazing!

Marlia Cochran, aka Marketing Morpheus. A huge shout out and thank you for sharing all of your marketing brilliance, helping me to wade through the minutiae of social media, listening and being a safe place for me to ask questions, giving constructive feedback, and always being ready with an idea. You rock!

Alyssa Coelho, aka Creative Direction and Design Avatar. Thank you for once again working your magic on the interior and cover design and using your special creative genius to bring it to life! You're the best! Thank you for adding your special touch to the interior, making the inside beautiful and easy to read.

To My Community...

To all of the early readers who previewed this book, a big thank you for reading this manuscript, giving me feedback, and sharing your amazing suggestions and great ideas. This book will forever wear your sweet touch and be better because of each one of you!

A special shout out to all of the moms who spent time reading it with or to your younger kiddos, asking them questions, and relaying their comments back to me. You have no idea how much you've blessed this book through your efforts.

With All My Love and Gratitude,

Mima (aka Lori)